SEE WHAT

"Though a novel, the storyline is optimistic about future reconciliation of faiths, yet resolute that the Christian faith stands alone with our one true God. Impressed and thankful to Dr. Carroll for the depth and intricacies about the various divisions of the Muslim faiths, and risks involved when one does seek out the True and Living LORD GOD!"

– Doreen Hung Mar, MD

Mission to the World Medical Associate Missionary

"Prince of the Sand is the best book of The Islamic Conflict Trilogy. In it, Dr. Carroll brings to bear his deep understanding of Islam, as well as of Middle East customs and politics, as he weaves together all the loose strands of the two previous books. The imagined future is bright and God is shown to be sovereign as he draws his people to himself in surprising ways and uses flawed humans to accomplish his will. Prince of the Sand portrays the inevitability of the triumph of the Kingdom of Jesus Christ. I highly recommend this book."

– Jerry A. Miller, Jr. MD

Author, *The Burden of Being Champ:*
The Dropout, The Legend, and The Pediatrician

"A riveting tale portraying the complex inner workings of private government circles, the fluctuating tensions between Sunni and Shia Muslims and the personal relationships affected in strained circumstances. In this third novel, you'll experience doubt, fear, joy and surprise as you delve into the detailed lives of each character and how God, above all, works in detailed, and often unseen, ways to change the hearts of the lost."

– John Kaddis, MD

US Physician, Raised in the Middle East

PRINCE
OF THE SAND

God Works in the Middle East

JIM CARROLL

HigherLife Development Services, Inc.

P.O. Box 623307

Oviedo, Florida 32762

(407) 563-4806

www.ahigherlife.com

Printed in Canada

10 9 8 7 6 5 4 3 2 1

Carroll, Jim

Prince of the Sand: God Works in the Middle East

Paperback: ISBN: 978-1-7337273-6-5

eBook: ISBN: 978-1-7337273-7-2

DEDICATION

I dedicate this novel to my family, who have endured and at times, even relished our forays into the Middle East.

This is a work of fiction. Although most of the history and *some* of the people are factual, names, characters, businesses, places, events, locales, and incidents are either the products of the author's imagination or used in a fictitious manner.

INTRODUCTION

When the missionary/evangelist "Apostle to Islam" Samuel Zwemer visited the Persian Gulf at the end of the nineteenth and early twentieth century, he thought the Muslims in the area were ripe for the gospel. By our timing, Zwemer was wrong. But God has His own timing. This third book of the Islamic Conflict Trilogy suggests what could happen even now. My story, really a prayer, delineates how God might bring about mass conversions in the area.

Another aspect of the account that follows proposes the onset of democracy. My Arab friends in Kuwait said to me many times, "The people of the Gulf aren't ready for democracy." Of course, there is no compulsory link between Christianity and democracy, but it is essential that there be no penalty for conversion from Islam to Christianity (known as apostasy, which today may carry severe punishment). Check out the story that follows and see how I suggest the Lord might solve this problem.

The main characters in the story are fictional, but the various Gulf leaders are based on real people. I had to guess which leader would still be alive at the time of the future events. The events themselves are a mix of history and fiction. The cultural aspects of the story are as close to reality as I could make them. In the face of ongoing news in the Gulf, I ask the reader to suspend disbelief for a time.

MAP OF THE MIDDLE EAST[1]

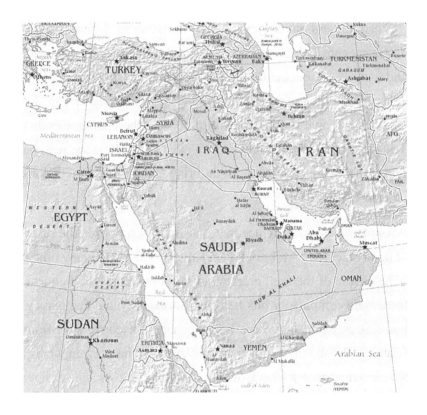

1 "Physical Map of the Middle East," Www.cia.gov/library/publications/resources/the-world-factbook/attachments/docs/original/middle_east.pdf?1528326232, accessed November 20, 2018, www.cia.gov/library/publications/resources/the-world-factbook/attachments/docs/original/middle_east.pdf?1528326232.

LIST OF CHARACTERS

Yusef: main character

Rabea: mother of Yusef. Rabea is dead by the time this story begins, but her influence over Yusef remains and still commands attention

Yacoub: Father of Yusef

Hibah: Sister of Yusef

Divina: Long-time Philippine maid of the family

Binyamin: Yusef's younger brother, a computer genius

Esau: Yusef's half-brother, declared enemy of the family and all religion

Thawab: Yusef's half-brother, eventually a leader in the Kuwaiti church

Tahara Al-Thani: Yusef's wife, member of the Qatari royal family

Fareed: Tahara's brother, husband of Hibah, instrumental in Gulf politics

Imam Ali Khatami: Shia cleric, Yusef's teacher in Shia theology

Afsin: young man saved by Yusef in earlier book

Sheikh Nawaf Al-Ahmad Al-Jaber Al-Sabah: Emir of Kuwait during the struggle

Karim Khadim: Yusef's former boss, director of Iranian Ministry of Economic Affairs and Finance

Anand Kulabali: Mysterious character who appears at critical times to help Yusef

Mohammad Zarif: Real Iranian diplomat, inserted in the story as the president of Iran

CHAPTER 1

OUR LOYAL ASSEMBLY

Every day during Kuwait's National Assembly parliamentary session, I drove north from Ahmadi along King Fahad bin Abdul Aziz Road to the too-large structure on Gulf Road with its roof sweeping upward in wings like a large, graceful bird, a mockery of reality. The spectacle was enhanced inside the building by the elevated visitors' gallery, half encircling us in our wooden desks on the assembly floor. Such was the setting I had been thrust into, not because of any merit of my own, but rather because of the circumstances related to my famous sojourning in Iranian prisons. I had gained office for reasons unconnected to my abilities or achievements. A hero without a heroic act. Had God visited this upon me for some purpose as yet unknown to me? Or was this just some joke of time and situation?

And as the first, the only Christian in Kuwait's Parliament, I felt the eyes of the spectators always focused on me. Somehow, I was deemed a star because of my imprisonment in Iran's dreadful Evin prison. But I was only a star to a few; to the rest, I was a target and had sustained many attempts on my life already. And here I was: home from my confinement in Iran and confined again in seemingly pointless, political harangues in a setting designed solely for the stability of the country's ruling elite. Although elected by the citizens, in reality we served at the pleasure of the emir. I became accustomed to the painful tension that was the order of each day for me, while my fellow members fed on the pressure they created, mostly for their own entertainment.

In the midst of this sustained brouhaha, Al-Hasawi's Islamist parliament coalition persisted in submitting bills designed to make the lives of non-Muslims in Kuwait more difficult. The list was long and varied: the prohibition of marriage of a Muslim to a non-Muslim, the prohibition of conversion of a Muslim to another religion, the requirement that all businesses have a Muslim partner of fifty-one percent, the requirement that all motor vehicles owned by Kuwaiti citizens have a Muslim as the primary owner, the requirement that all property in Kuwait be owned only by Muslims, and finally that no buildings could be used for worship by non-Muslims. The bill prohibiting the conversion of a Muslim was particularly interesting in that they did not propose the death penalty for "apostasy" but the removal of all property rights instead.

The months of March and April, 2022, were consumed by debate of these bills. As the lone Christian in the Parliament, I was placed in the strenuous position of having to enter the fray on nearly every bill. The principle behind most of these bills was to deprive Kuwaiti Christians of their means of economic sustainment and social progress. The Kuwaiti Parliament building with its winglike up-slanted roof design assumed the shape of a physical launching pad for insults sent up to Jesus:

"We cannot allow Christians to flourish in Kuwait."

"Rich Kuwaiti Christians will overrun Kuwait."

"We've seen enough of the damage these people can do."

Through this rancor, I greeted my colleagues and smiled. I wore extra deodorant, unlike my associates, who, I suspected, wore none. My sister, Hibah, said the ordeal was making me smell bad. I was jumpy, anxious about everything, and lost ten pounds.

Support of my position against these bills came from an unexpected quarter. The small Shia coalition saw the proposals as an assault on the economic freedom of a minority other than themselves. One approached me between sessions. "Yusef, you've got to protect us. We know we're next." They were fearful that such a trend could be part of a pattern that could bleed over and affect their own position in the social structure. While the Shias in Kuwait were generally silent and accepting of their lesser position, they did not want any further erosion of their status. What an odd alliance: Shia and Christian. Perhaps there was something to it. Even as I thought this, I dismissed idea. How could there be an alliance between those who know Jesus and those who don't?

The Sunni were, by far, the largest group of Muslim believers. Only about twenty percent followed Shia Islam. Though both adhered to the dictates of Muhammad, they disagreed on the succession of leaders and other factors surrounding their authority and ability. Their most notable differences were found in the Shia foundational belief that theirs was the purest Islam of all, and that their Mahdi, a redeemer, had already been born and would return, fight, and conquer all evil to save them. This idea had parallels to the Christian view of the return of Christ, except that the Shia believed Jesus would be with this Mahdi when he returned. Although related, these ideas could not logically coexist. Even though the Shia believed in the return of Jesus as a man, they did not see him as God himself.

Nevertheless, I was appreciative of their support. Two Shia colleagues invited me for a coffee at a restaurant near the parliament, and we sat together comfortably. "What's it like to be a Christian?" one asked.

"It's like being in a fishbowl with bigger fish."

They laughed at my little joke and nodded.

"Yes, we know about that." This was first time I had a relaxed conversation with any Shia without an agenda. Was there any room for a genuine alliance?

I gained insight in the grouping of Shia versus Sunni in a physical way: Mercedes versus Chevrolet Caprice, still the most popular car made now made especially for the Middle East. Wow! I could tell one from another by the parking lot!

After all this nonsense, only one of the bills passed: that Muslims own all property in Kuwait. Had this been enforced, the property of my family and that of all Kuwaiti Christians would have been seized by the government. The emir quashed the law based on the technical fact that there was no method by which the property could be taken and no agency designated to re-as-sign that property. I received a note from Emir Nawaf: "Yusef, on some things I am still with you." Did that mean in other areas he was not with me? Why did the emir even bother to contact me?

The time of my term in parliament sailed by in the midst of these small squabbles on the floor of the grand building, alternating with the strange, developing friendships with my Shia colleagues. These things I could take in stride.

CHAPTER 2

WILL THERE BE MUSIC IN DOHA?

But the routine was interrupted. The emir assigned to me to a meeting in Doha, Qatar for the approval of a joint educational project between our two states, apparently a harmless deputation for a Christian—no way I could cause the emir any trouble on this assignment. And at least for the time out of Kuwait, I would be safe from the ongoing physical threats toward me.

The emir invited five of us to the palace for a briefing about the Qatar visit. In addition to myself, there was Siddiqah Al-Humaidi, Hamdan Al-Khalid, Fadi Al-Naqeeb, and Ri'ad Al-Hasawi. Al-Humaidi was from the College of Education at Kuwait University and the daughter of a prominent local Shia cleric. Al-Khalid was a longtime member of parliament and known for his spirit of moderation. Al-Naqeeb was a well-off businessman involved in imports and exports, some of them even legal. He was a relative of the emir. His choice reflected the general concern among those in international commerce that regional conflicts of any sort could have adverse effects on their income. And disturbing to many was that this was already being felt, or at least imagined. Al-Hasawi was the former opponent with whom I had had many debates in the recent election. Both of us had been elected. I was uncertain why he was selected for the commission, but then my own selection was also surprising. The only reason I could think of was that it had to do with my being a Christian, but that single fact actually made my participation quite delicate.

The elderly emir was gracious in receiving us, and made a ceremony of the first part of our visit with TV cameras present. The camera panned around the room at our obedient, smiling faces, each with our hands clasped in front. I was the only one dressed in a Western suit, gray Armani.

"First, I want to thank you for agreeing to serve in this function." There was really little choice.

"Next, let me discuss the educational aspects of your mission. I know you're aware Qatar has what they have named Education City, which is a center for a number of Western university branches in collaboration with Qatar University. This arrangement has afforded them considerable flexibility in offering a wide variety of educational opportunities. I would like you to discuss our integration into the "City" in trade for their students having the opportunity to study at Kuwait University. This will be a happy arrangement for our young citizens and for the Gulf as a whole." He dismissed the camera operatives at this point.

After the cameras were gone, he went on to the real reason for the conference. There was an awkward silence as the newspeople filed out.

Emir Nawaf was eighty-five years old. We all knew he tired

easily, and he was anxious to get through the instructions. Still, they were remarkably detailed. As he gestured to us, we observed his bony, thin-skinned fingers, the excessive bruising on the fragile skin of his forearms. How much longer would this old man be able to go on as he did?

"The details of the educational arrangement have already been worked out at a higher level, and your purpose is to give face to the proceedings. I don't think the educational discussion will require more than a day."

Then the tripwire: the Shia issue vaulting into the foreground, my relaxation vanished. "The more important purpose for your visit is to engage the biggest problem we are experiencing in the Muslim world—that Sunni and Shia no longer live together in peace. This schism is causing economic unbalance." By this he meant Sunnis were being hurt financially, and the conflict was already far beyond the discussion stage. Shia Iran had developed alliances with Russia, both countries supporting the Houthis and their fiasco of a revolt in Yemen. The Houthis were a Zaidi sect of Shias, which had arisen in opposition to former Yemen president, Ali Abdullah Saleh. Saudi Arabia had aligned with the other Sunni states (and remarkably with Israel) against the Shia in Yemen, formerly the land of the queen of Sheba. The Sunni-Shia mess was complex and long out of control, and I was now being dumped into this mess. "I'm therefore asking you to begin discussions with several individuals, chosen by them, from their side of the conflict." We exchanged glances among ourselves. The common thought among us? *Oh no, not this again, not the Sunni-Shia conflict. And what will we have to contribute?* We all knew the answer in advance.

Qatar was one of two Arab countries, the other being Saudi Arabia, which held primarily to a strictly conservative Wahhabi/Salafi tradition. No useful dialogue could be carried out in that setting. Even more peculiar was the fact that Saudi Arabia had assigned Qatar to the status of an adversary, making them the current albatross of the Gulf. Was this due to some unusual Qatari relationship with Iran, or just political wrangling? Little Kuwait still desired to remain aloof from this quagmire.

The talks about the Sunni/Shia conflict were scheduled to begin the day after the educational matter, and were to occur in the Educational City as a cover for their real purpose.

But there was more in the visit for me. Following my election to parliament, I had endured interviews from a number of news outlets about my status as the first Christian elected to parliament in Kuwait. Most of these had been painful and pointless, but one, from Al Jazeera, still arrested my continuing attention. The interviewer, Tahara Al-Thani, had caught me off guard, not only with her incisive questions, but also with her startling good looks and direct eye contact. As she closed the session, she had also suggested I contact her if I ever came to Doha. Never before had such a thing happened to me with an Arab woman.

###

And now, as if by predestination (pardon the religious word), I was going to Doha. Our group arrived January 20, 2022 as the news was breaking that ISIL fighters were again on the outskirts of Baghdad and threatening Shia areas, just as they had been periodically over the years. The United States tried air strikes, seeming not to understand that all air strikes accomplished was to redirect the course of the battle to other areas. I thought of the whack-a-mole game. Every time you whacked your enemy, he popped up somewhere else. You could never beat him.

We lodged in the Grand Heritage Hotel Doha near the education complex. Before I unpacked my bag, I searched the local Al Jazeera website for Tahara Al-Thani. I phoned their office, reached her line and left a message: "Hello, Ms. Al-Thani, I'm staying at the Grand Heritage for a meeting. Perhaps we could speak." I left my cell number. It seemed as if all had been decided. My heart beat faster for a moment.

The next day was just as expected: a discussion with the representatives of the educational project. We exchanged cordial talk for two hours and concluded that the agreement between Qatar and Kuwait would proceed as had already been established. In effect the agreement was meaningless as such exchanges for students were already occurring. It was pointless, except as a covering for the real purpose of our trip.

During the meeting, a text came to my phone, "I'll come for you tonight in the lobby at seven. Tahara."

That night she greeted me in the hotel lobby. She was dressed in a black Gucci suit. I was stunned. "Good evening, Yusef! I'm glad you told me of your arrival. I want to show you some of our country." Her white Mercedes was waiting in the hotel greeting area where parking was not permitted; her family privilege was obvious. Getting in, she drove to the area known as the Pearl of Qatar, the ever-expanding cultural center of Qatar. The Pearl was an artificial island on which were constructed upscale residences, hotels, markets, parks, and restaurants. The island was circular with a lagoon in its center and multiple extensions branching out into the Gulf.

"We've nothing like this in Kuwait. Qatar has certainly sur-passed us in building."

"Well, it's all just money and things. There's little else behind it. I heard you were here to develop some sort of educational cooper-ation project. How's that coming?" We parked in an area marked "Police Only." Privilege has its perks.

"The discussion has been completed."

"But you're here for several more days."

"Yes, there's another reason for our visit. But if I tell you about it, our talk must be strictly off-the-record." She smiled and nod-ded in agreement. "My involvement here makes no sense to me, but then none of us in our group understand.. The emir of Kuwait and the emir of Qatar want to initiate discussion on the Sunni/ Shia conflict. Our emir says he wants us to look for some basis of agreement. We must give him credit for that desire. Some of the issue is religious, and you know the story there, but the bulk of it is political and fueled by a desire to maintain the status quo for those with the power, land, and money. So, there are really several levels of discussion. It wasn't stated which level we're to pursue, but it's probably the religious framework, which doesn't seem in the top rank. Only one member of our team is Shia, and as you know, I'm a Christian. My sister Hibah said you were a Christian too. I don't know how she knew that."

"Yes, I am. She and I had a little time for off-the-record discussion. All very interesting, don't you think? The Lord is organizing the symphony. I think any successful harmony of the Sunni/Shia conflict would lead to the dissolution of the whole Islamic theology. The Sunni depend on the wisdom of the community and the Shia on divine inspiration." We walked along the side of the concrete island on the new cobblestone path. I worried about her high heels as they clacked on the uneven surface.

"You're way ahead of me on this line of thinking. I'm still intrigued about your family name, Al Thani."

"Emir Sheikh Tamim bin Hamad Al Thani, is my second cousin. Other than the name itself, it means little or nothing." That was not true, as demonstrated by her parking habits. "I don't know how many Al-Thanis there are in Qatar."

"I've wondered about Al Jazeera. What's the story with that? I know that when it first began, the news network led to the UAE, Saudi Arabia, and Bahrain recalling their ambassadors from Qatar and to a split in the Gulf Cooperation Council." The GCC, though still functioning in name, was mostly impotent.

"Sheikh Hamad bin Khalifa Al Thani provided a loan of nearly $150 million in 1996 in order to get the news company rolling. You're wondering what the motivation was and whether there is an unspoken agenda. The answer is yes, there is. The reasons are both complicated and simple. Ostensibly, Al Jazeera was put in place as an eastern alternative to CNN. That's definitely a good thing, by any measure. You've probably seen the deterioration of CNN these days. The news they offer is either made to seem terribly funny, sensationalized, or they repeat it every thirty minutes *ad nauseum*. Opinion is presented as news. Al Jazeera, on the other hand, has worked hard to maintain a sense of factual reporting and a concentrated effort to be serious about serious matters with a clear separation of fact and opinion. I think that's apparent from seeing the Al Jazeera product. I regret we had to move our efforts out of the United States, but we were not wanted there."

"However, there is another agenda—one you probably won't believe. It's subterranean. As far as the emir who started Al Jazeera was concerned, his motivation was just what I mentioned, but there were others that had urged him to start Al Jazeera in my family, who had a long-term plan. Their idea was that it could be a format for honest reporting on Christianity in the Arab world. To some extent that sort of reporting has come to fruition. But the rest of the plan is still ahead, perhaps years ahead. The hope, the intention of those in my family who influenced the emir, was that Al Jazeera would become the voice of believers in the Gulf, and indeed, in the Muslim world. The emir himself was not aware what he was starting, and there it is—believe it or not."

I was silent for a time. What had I gotten myself into? This exposure was completely outside my thinking. Once again God had jumped into territory where He was not welcome. Why did He keep doing that?

By this time, we had strolled along the walkway of the Pearl for some time, the clear waters of the Gulf lapping at our left. Of the many restaurants, we settled in an Argentinian establishment that specialized in steaks. In my mind women usually did not prefer steak, but this was Tahara's choice. We took a table as near the sea as possible. When he saw Tahara, the maître-de gave us special attention. The decorations were leather, all browns and dull orange, and the light bulbs peered through thin leather lampshades. The result was a golden glow. She ordered a large T-bone, rare, which I duplicated. There was classical guitar music in the background, not the eleven-stringed *oud* we would have heard in Kuwait.

Tahara went on with the story, "My father was a Christian. He was converted as a young adult. He had already married by the time he converted, and his wife was Muslim. My father is dead. He died two years ago. My mother lives and she's still covered. Of course, we're praying for her, but the Lord has not yet answered. My father's conversion began with a dream. He became curious after the dream and read the Bible. He had already memorized the Quran as a youth, and the clarity and linear scope of the Scriptures in comparison was a shock to him." Tahara teared up for a moment as she recalled her father. I put my hand on her forearm for a second and then removed it, not wanting to abridge decorum.

17

"This was all maybe twenty-five years ago. He was one of the first Muslim converts of Qatar. He taught me and saw that I took Jesus as my Savior. I'd like to say my father was responsible for the conversion of Qataris, but of course the Lord is the One who is responsible. The same story or a variation of it has occurred many times here."

I followed with my family's story, and I had to give credit to my mother. "My mother was the most amazing person I've ever known. She had little formal schooling, but was brilliant, full of wisdom, probing in her intellect, often to my pain and discomfort."

"Is she the one who pointed you to Jesus?"

"Yes, there's no question about that." I think Tahara expected me to elablorate, but I was paralyzed in the moment. I saw this Shia-Sunni thing becoming increasingly complex and even dangerous. How, why, had God put all this together, inserting me into situatuons too intricate for me to grasp? I compared my standing before God with what I saw in my mother. While I did have faith, it didn't measure up to the standard set by her in my estimate, and I feared my deficiencies would be detected. There were moments I fully trusted, and then my feeble heart intervened. I still had the fear that someone would probe my faith too closely. So, I was silent.

But Tahara was more confident than I expected. She reminded me of Hibah. No wonder they had bonded so quickly. She finished her steak and soaked up the bloody gravy with her bread. I could not finish the large piece of meat. We listened to the music for a while and drank a Turkish coffee. Then we walked back to her car, and she delivered me back to the hotel. I was uncertain about where our meeting would lead, but I said, "I'll phone you as soon as I can."

I couldn't sleep that night. My lack of sleep gave me time to question everything.

The next morning, we began the Sunni-Shia discussion, and everything in me wanted to be elsewhere, anywhere. The representatives from Doha were all clerics of varying degrees of seniority, about half Sunni and half Shia, and they all outdistanced the Kuwaiti delegation in religious knowledge. One of the Shia from Qatar, Hussein Al-Husseini, announced he had been named discussion leader by the emir. Al-Husseini began the meeting by stating the agenda, saying, "I propose this as a tentative schedule. First, a review of the Shia theological position, second, a review of the Sunni theological position, next, a path to theological reconciliation, and finally, other necessary paths." With the stated agenda, the mood in the room sank further into boredom. All but me had heard all this many times, and I didn't want to suffer through it.

Al-Husseini led the first portion. He spoke for four hours. His central theme was victimization by those who sought power. "Ali, the true heir of Mohammed, was first put aside and did not assume the rightful leadership of Islam until twenty-four years after the death of Mohammed. Hussein, the son of Ali and therefore the leader designated by Allah, was martyred, taken from us, in Karbala along with many of his followers, sixty-one years after the Prophet's departure from Mecca to Medina, or in the year 680 as the Christians call it; and the rightful spiritual leadership of Islam was cut off. The subsequent twelve inspired imams have languished without proper rights and authority afforded to them. The twelfth imam today lives, but is unknown. Our authority has rested in the appointment of these twelve imams chosen by Allah. Our authority is not from man." The room was too large for the group, and Husseini's voice echoed in the hall. At some point, the air conditioner failed and we were all sweating. By the time he had finished, half his audience was asleep. One of the Qataris was snoring. Everyone but me knew this history already, and I had avoided most of it in my Christian worldview. We were awakened by the silence that took over when he stopped speaking. He looked about the room proudly.

A two-hour lunch ensued with fried zubaidi , a Gulf fish that looks like a freshwater bream, grilled tomatoes and french fries. We ate slowly so as not to get back to the meeting any sooner than necessary. The lunch lasted until three, and at the resumption of the meeting, Al-Husseini announced we would adjourn for the day. I gave quiet thanks.

The next morning Al-Hasawi gave the likewise unnecessary recitation of Sunni theology. He spoke only for an hour, and ended with the statement, "The authority in Sunni Islam is the combined wisdom of the overall community and the wisest of the community. Our leaders make decisions based on our glorious history and the united (and best) thoughts of our people." He was not a student of theology, and his presentation lacked depth, for which I was grateful. The conferees persisted with glum, determined faces.

Immediately following the Sunni presentation, an awkward struggle erupted in the back of the auditorium between two of the Qatari participants: one Sunni, the other Shia. The ungainly turning, grappling, and puffing of the two unskilled, overweight combatants obscured the seriousness of the altercation. The Shia's previously concealed knife was soon discovered embedded in the abdomen of the Sunni. We called the emergency line. All of us were unaccustomed to so much blood, and we didn't know how to proceed.

"Should we pull out the knife?'

"That might make the bleeding worse."

"I think the fat is stopping the bleeding."

After conferring, we decided to leave the knife implanted in the poor man's abdomen.

The Shia sat in the corner, holding his bowed head on his knees, sobbing. Before the police and ambulance arrived, both men were interrogated by Al-Husseini.

"What is the reason for this awful thing? What will our Kuwaiti friends think?"

At first the Shia said he been offended by the discussion of Sunni theology. How had the discussion been reduced to knives and blood so quickly? But then the real reason for the conflict came out.

The Shia sobbed, "The pig took my wife. She, whom I loved,

who lived in my house, has left from under my roof and now is the wife of this swine. He has no regard for a man's wife and no regard for Islam. He is an adulterer and an apostate."

The Shia was taken off to jail and the Sunni to the hospital, where, we were informed, he survived. The knife did not penetrate the abdominal cavity. The thick abdominal fat pad had absorbed the entire knife blade.

And so another day was spent.

I phoned Tahara, and she asked me to her home for dinner. She sent a car to pick me up at the hotel. The driver was Pakistani, and we chatted about the latest cricket match in Islamabad. I was nervous, no, downright scared. We drove for thirty minutes to Al-Wakrah just south of Doha. Her home was by the sea. I was ushered into the living room by the female Indian servant; and after sitting down, I was joined by Tahara's older brother, Fareed. I was to be vetted.

I looked about the room. The surroundings were not at all like the typical Arab home, but more like my father's in Ahmadi. The furniture was of good quality and functional, but not ornate. There was no plastic cover on the couch, which indicated the room was actually used by the family. There were Bibles and assorted Bible commentaries on a small bookshelf, and tons of photos of family members, men, uncovered women, and children. One of the group photographs included the smiling Qatari emir. Even with the possible challenge from the brother sitting across from me, I was enveloped in the warmth of the home.

"Yusef, I understand you're on a committee to resolve the Sunni-Shia conflict," he smiled. Fareed was forty-five, half-bald, clean-shaven and about twenty-five pounds overweight. I thought of the old Arab saying: "A man without a beard is like a rat without a tail." What was coming next? What was he thinking? His expression betrayed no hint of his next words. He seemed like a good guy, who had been placed in the awkward position of talking to me about marrying his sister, or so I thought.

I answered, "I find my role in this Sunni-Shia thing strange, even pointless." I wanted out of this conflict before it worsened.

"Well, there may be a greater purpose. We must assume that. Tell me about your incarceration in Iran. How did you ever make it?"

What an odd place to kick off our first conversation. Was this question a well-conceived aim to probe the depth of my faith? "I came through it with the Lord's help, though there were times when I doubted the outcome."

"Who wouldn't have had doubts? I'd like to hear about them."

"I doubted everything at times, both God and myself. I'm still not over it." His calm manner and kind smile had forced me to be honest. He didn't wince at my answer.

"Yusef, we know much about your family and the Christian movement in Kuwait. There are many similarities to our brief Christian history here in Qatar. I'll be very clear. We believe God has chosen you for His own purposes." This was starting to sound like a job interview. Was there more in play than the marriage? "Everyone has noted your public charisma. You don't need to look down. You know the truth in what I'm saying. We need you to fill out God's greater purpose for you. You don't yet have the quiet heart of a faithful servant. God has not gotten you ready yet. You know that, and so do the rest of us. Your sister has informed on you. But in His time you will have that." *How could he be so certain that my reluctance would dissipate?* "And as you have certainly ascertained, my sister has asked that I speak with you. She'll be here soon." I understood the part about Tahara, but not about my being "chosen" to do anything. Here I was in Qatar for this Sunni-Shia thing (against my will) and now the suggestion of some more involved, more intense role was being suggested. My first thought? *No way!*

I had thought the vetting was solely for marriage, but Fareed had added the layer of something else. Who was this *we* Fareed referred to when he spoke? What was the *greater purpose*? My fears surfaced again. *I was done with any greater purpose.* What was God thinking when he put me in this situation? I prayed: "Answer me when I call, O God of my righteousness! You have given me relief when I was in distress. Be gracious to me and hear my prayer!"(Psalm 4:1). My prayer was childishly brief. Perhaps my call failed to go through.

As those questions opened in my mind, Tahara entered the room with the announcement that dinner was served. She looked beautiful in a dazzlingly white suit, and her understated perfume followed her. I knew my future was decided in that moment.

We sat at the large table with the extended family, fourteen in total. Tahara was on my left. Fareed gave thanks and we embarked on the typical Arab family meal of many dishes, much more than could be consumed at one sitting. The fresh hamour, more properly known as the brown-spotted reef cod, was especially good. The quail was also a treat. The quail brought to my mind Mahfouz's novel, *Autumn Quail*, one of my father's favorites that centered on the moral responsibility of a corrupt young man. Strange it would come to me then. My father's influence?

Once again, Tahara's appetite surprised me. She ate quickly and with great enjoyment.

The close of the meal would normally be the typical time for the departure of guests in an Arab home, but Fareed made it clear I was to remain so that he and I could talk again.

We adjourned to the living room once more. "Yusef, I'm sure you're mystified by the events of the evening. You're wondering where it's all heading. First, Tahara. I must apologize for being involved here, but our father is dead, and we still follow the Arab model to some degree. Your sister, Hibah, contacted Tahara and proposed the match. Your little committee visit to Qatar provided opportunity for further assessment. I have yet to get Tahara's final thoughts, but I've seen how you look at her. So, I trust you and she will deal with whatever course remains. For what it's worth, I approve." All this was familiar to me as an Arab, but still it seemed odd. A bit cold but necessary.

"But then, the other matter."

"I thought we were only talking about Tahara and me. Now I'm dense on what you're getting at."

"It will take some time for me to even know how to be clear. But the movement of believers here in the Gulf is growing and moving quickly, albeit quietly. All of us hope it will happen without the shedding of too much blood. But *'in shā' Allāh* (as God wills). All the countries of the Gulf, to a greater or lesser degree, are involved. We have representatives in each one." Once again, the *we*. "The knowledge of their names is compartmentalized for now for their safety. There are several parts to the movement. Of course, there's the purely religious which deals with evangelism, conversion, and spiritual growth. Yes, Yusef, I see you look incredulous. I'm talking about how the gospel will spread. Then, there are legal issues. We must deal with possible penalties for so-called apostasy. Next there is publicity or public relations, and the control of news flow. We need to develop stronger military contacts. We all hope that's not needed, but we must be prepared. We also need stronger elements in the government of the various Gulf States. Finally, we must keep the financial needs of the movement in mind."

What was all this? I felt dizzy. This *we* business. Fareed was moving too fast for me to keep up. Why was I hearing all this?

"You will lead us. Not yet, but in the future, perhaps soon, perhaps not so soon; we will need a face of leadership. That will be you. You've been identified as the one to take this role." *Surely I deserved more voice in this.*

26

I was suddenly ill, overwhelmed both physically and spiritually. *Who had identified me? Was there a prophet? How did Fareed have the authority to say these things?*

But whatever else Fareed was talking about, I was delighted about the possibility of marrying Tahara. The choice would be hers. But the issues now being addressed by Fareed seemed completely outside the boundaries of reality. Fareed had already identified my spiritual shortcoming. Still, he told me of my anticipated role. My faith was not sufficient for my trouble. My earlier Iran fiasco left me believing I was finished with any more testing. But I did know from these experience that the Lord never quits.

Was Fareed talking about a concept or a real organization?

I still thought I was an outsider. "I have become a stranger to my brothers, an alien to my mother's sons" (Psalm 69:8). This psalm reminded me I was not up to the task set before me.

"What will happen next?"

"I'll call Tahara to come down and drive you back to the hotel. Whatever happens is between the two of you. About the other, you won't hear anything for a while, perhaps even a year or two, but you will indeed hear. As the Americans put it, this is all on a *need-to-know* basis." If I was to be the leader, why wasn't I being told more?

Fareed sent word via the servant and Tahara soon appeared.

We proceeded to her car for the drive back to my hotel. I was paralyzed; whether from her presence next to me or the news

I had received, I couldn't say. Here I was next to this beautiful woman who wanted to marry me, and I couldn't speak. Tahara was driving and couldn't make sustained eye contact with me. We first exchanged pleasantries and then there was silence. She certainly was aware of the content of her brother's conversation with me, but the prelude to our apparent or supposed relationship had been too short. I needed time to think it through. I wasn't quick about all the emotional stuff, and time was slipping away. I couldn't sustain the superficial aspects of the conversation, and we fell into a complete hush. Her posture stiffened as we neared my hotel. She pulled up in the portico. "Well, Yusef, I hope you had a pleasant evening." There was a sarcastic tone, and I got out and went through the revolving door of the hotel, passing through the metal detector.

I was aghast. What a fool I was! She expected words of love from me and I sat there like a robot. Had I blown it? I saw the future without Tahara. I fumbled for my phone. "Tahara, please come back."

Within five minutes she was back in the hotel driveway.

I jumped in front of the doorman, who gasped as I pushed him out of the way in my effort to open her door first. Before even getting into the car, all I could say was, "Tahara, will you marry me?" The doorman was aghast at my impropriety.

She was direct. "Yes, Yusef."

The icy atmosphere in the car was gone, and we drove down to the Pearl for a walk. We walked for hours, holding hands, daring any watchers to restrain us. What had happened? We knew we had to be careful about too much public affection, but an Al-Thani was apparently privileged, even in this. There was a set of miracles in front of us. We stopped at a coffee shop, and there was soft Western jazz. The music carried us both to a place where only the musicians knew the direction of the melody, and we were swept along as if in a sea current. The world had changed, and there were now plans to make. How strange the day! Time spun out of my control. Events proceeded faster than I could act. What should I do next? I had no idea. I thought my loss of control was only temporary, for I had a way of taking control, but I was wrong.

The Shia-Sunni conference convened again the next morning with the two Qatari combatants replaced by another two clerics. Our topic was theological reconciliation. After two hours, we agreed that the Quran was acceptable to both sides. The fact that even this level of agreement was not immediate indicated the width of the chasm to be breached. After four more hours, we agreed it was impossible to come together on all the *hadiths* (the sayings of the Prophet Muhammed) as they differed between the two sides. But perhaps there was a body of hadiths that could be accepted by both. The Qatari clerics agreed to research this possibility and report back. But the main point of disagreement was authority—whether the divinely inspired Shia imam or the summation of the wisdom of the Sunni community had the last word. Al-Husseini concluded we could not solve this issue in the current venue, and we moved on. Finally, he was on point.

The final matter for our group was the question about other areas of necessary reconciliation. These were the same concerns expressed by any minority to the majority—the financial, political, and social repercussions of being different. Worldwide, Shias comprised about twenty percent of all Muslims. They were the minority in most countries. We concluded we should refer this concern to the attention of the governments of the various countries. The financial gap was wide between them, with the Shia having far fewer resources.

We were left with the theological differences, and we did not know where to turn on that question. None of our participants, even the Qatari clerics, had sufficient theological credentials to carry weight in this discussion. The conference ended with the expected result. Both emirs would be satisfied by the lack of a conclusive position. A vigorous decision could be dangerous to all parties.

Tahara and I met again briefly before I flew back to Kuwait. The music of Doha returned home with me. What changes would it bring?

CHAPTER 3

SWEPT BY EVENTS

Hibah met me and swept me up in both her arms at the airport. She and Tahara had spoken by phone before I arrived, and Hibah was beaming. Every time I looked at her, the smile was there. The two women had already agreed the wedding would take place in May 2022 in Doha, and there was no need to consult me. I was only the groom. As Tahara drove me back to Ahmadi, her excitement continued, and she drove too fast for the heavy traffic—130 km/h—talking at a rapid rate the entire time. "Yusef, it's going to be the biggest wedding in the history of the Gulf." She was not usually given to hyperbole. All I wanted was to get married, and I appreciated that the arrangements were removed from my hands.

The outcome of my official visit to Qatar remained uncertain and unresolved, and I couldn't put the pieces together. First, there was the report we were obligated to make to the emir; the truth was that the Sunni-Shia conference had achieved nothing. Thus, I faced another dreaded meeting with a meaningless outcome.

The emir convened our committee the next morning. We plastered smiles on our faces, and my cheeks ached with the forced levity. Al-Hasawi reported the events of the meeting accurately, but with the overall interpretation that the result was successful.

This was a necessity for meeting with the emir. This twist was difficult, but Hasawi managed it with considerable skill. We were all thankful he skipped the knife fight.

The emir smiled and understood the truth—that the Sunni-Shia conference had accomplished little. He had expected nothing from us, and he wanted nothing more. The meeting had achieved a diplomatic pleasantry with the Qatari emir; therefore all was well in emir-dom.

Our committee was given the thanks of a grateful Kuwait and discharged from this specific service. Al-Hasawi was rewarded by the public thanks of the emir before the parliament. Nawaf showed his white false teeth in a broad smile for the cameras as the education cooperative project was explained. Newspaper reports glowed. The Shia-Sunni subject would surface again at the proper time, but only when there were no other choices and nothing left to impede the rising conflict. With my marriage in view, I had no desire to face it.

The next evening, my father and I sat in our Ahmadi home garden, still maintained as my mother had planted it many years before. I told him about the double-barreled vetting episode as it had occurred with Fareed. "Yusef, don't let yourself be overwhelmed by this. The Lord is in control. Don't wonder why you've become the focal point. It has little to do with you. You might be the instrument, but that's all." My father a prophet? For a brief moment I resented the idea I was being used. No, actually it was longer than a moment.

"Yes, I want to marry Tahara, but I have no desire for any new quest—whatever the purpose. Someone else can take the leadership role. If God is in control, then why I am needed anyway? If it's as you portray, He can choose anyone."

"He designed you for this time, with all your grace and beauty and charm, and, of course, your flaws, which have been amply exposed. I don't think anything will happen for a while. You'll marry in the spring; and if the Lord blesses you, He may give you a year before you're called to battle."

But the respite was brief. Preparation for the marriage vaulted into the sphere of diplomatic and religious diplomacy.

The wedding was set in Qatar for mid-May. The complicating feature was that Tahara was both a Christian and a member of the royal family. In addition, the Al-Tamimis, my family, were known throughout the Gulf for their longstanding business prominence, as well as the "cowardly" departure of my father from Kuwait during the first Iraq war, and now for my recent imprisonment in Iran and newfound political prominence. Oddly enough, my imprisonment in Iran had conferred upon me a heroic status, even in the Gulf at large, at least on the western shore of the sea. Perhaps I should have gloried in the light shined on me, but I wished for anonymity. Now, I saw that the wedding would be attended and reported by local news agencies and certainly by Al Jazeera.

No question, the real complication was the fact that Tahara and I were Christians. This was well known in Kuwait for the Al-Tamimi family. But for the Al-Thanis of Qatar, the religious status of Tahara could generate significant complications for the emir. He was certainly aware of her Christian testimony, but it could be catastrophic for his authority if the information were disseminated. The religious issue placed a cloud over the wedding.

Tahara was unperturbed. We spoke by phone. "Yusef, don't worry. Our emir will cover all this." How was that possible? She and Hibah remained confident.

The customary Qatari social aspects of the wedding were not a problem for us. We could still celebrate with all the delightful accoutrements of the typical Gulf Arab wedding.

The chief obstacle was the legal one. The specific requirement for a Muslim marriage is that the marriage contract be stated in terms of Islamic law. Even though he knew we were both Christians, the emir insisted upon such a "Muslim" contract. Without it, the legality of the union would be in question, and he would be politically vulnerable. Therefore, the emir appealed to the judge of the Sharia court that had to approve the contract.

Tahara related the outcome to me by phone. The Sharia judge, with the knowledge that my family was Christian, told the emir he would not officiate the union.

"This man is no longer Sharia judge. He may go to his house and see his wife," replied the emir. The *former* judge should have expected this response. Another judge, more agreeable to the concerns of the emir, was quickly located and appointed.

The signing of the marriage contract constitutes the official marriage itself, and is completed long before the wedding celebration. While the marriage may be consummated at this legal point, it was usually delayed until after the celebration. Such was to be the case for our union.

I went to Qatar in late February 2022 for the signing. The Sharia court was located on Al Rayyan Road near Mannai Ra in the Musherib area. I was driven in the family S-Class Mercedes from the airport. We picked up Tahara, and she and I sat in the back seat with the middle seat vacant between us. We were both stiff, hands folded. Why were we so rigid? We must have appeared as though we were headed for the gallows. We arrived at the assigned time, and Fareed met us, accompanied by two close friends, both Christians, to be the required witnesses of the contract or *nikah*, as it is called. The judge was serious and fast in his actions. Five minutes passed and the work was complete. The judge was, in fact, a prisoner. If he wanted to continue as a Sharia judge in Qatar, he had to do this to please the emir. From my own experiences, I was sympathetic to his plight.

For the *mahr* or marriage gift I brought the gold my mother had stolen from her mother when she was married off as a child to my father. I presented the gift to Tahara in a red, leather-covered box, designed to simulate the containers formerly used on desert caravans for camels to bear goods. Somehow the gift seemed a completion of poetic justice. The gold had been stolen from a parent who allowed her child to be married to a full-grown man, my father, and now the gold was given to one who was making the choice of her own free will instead.

The signatories did their duty, and the contract was completed. The signing was a serious occasion, and the grim surroundings of the court reflected that solemnity. The office secretary looked on, her fingers supporting her chin. Following the signing, Tahara and I had dinner together as a married couple on the Pearl—again at the Argentinian restaurant. How could a woman consume such a large piece of meat? Hungering to be joined, we lingered over the meal for two hours. We said goodbye to each other and proceeded to our individual vehicles. We did not consummate the marriage, planning to wait until after the marriage celebration. We had barely touched. I flew back to Kuwait that evening and did not see Tahara again until the celebration in May. A legal marriage in a courtroom, and then nothing for three months.

What did all this mean for me—both the marriage and the strange exchange with her brother, Fareed, about my future role? Could I have the first and avoid the second? Did I have a choice at all? I was on a search, but for what?

The news that a prominent Kuwaiti family would marry into the Qatari royal family brought out the local Kuwait news agencies. The marriage, coupled with my seat in the parliament, almost led to the forgiveness of my Christianity. There were others, however, who saw the combination as a danger and an insult to Islam. An Internet blog appeared with this contention. *The approaching marriage of a known Kuwaiti Christian into the royal family of Qatar can only be viewed as symptomatic of the deterioration of the Islamic morals and ethics of our Gulf society. This whole affair is an invasion into the stability of our governments and fami-*

lies. As a general principle, we abhor the use of violence to defend the values of our society; but if violence is the only solution, and here we know of no other remedy, then we should do what is necessary to purge the unbeliever from his place of prominence. The identity of the blogger was at first obscure, but in time my younger brother, Binyamin, identified Esau as the author. Esau had been at odds with our family for a long time. How could Esau reclaim his role as our enemy, especially since he had been deported for crimes against Kuwait?

Esau, my half-brother, the product of my father's affair during his graduate school days, still considered me and the rest of our family as targets of revenge. Now he was acting against us—even while he was outside of Kuwait.

We could only hope Esau did not have the courage, intention, or means to pursue his recommendation, but there were others who would relish the task. I had already been assaulted, and I knew it could happen again, but there was little I could do as a precaution. I was thankful to the emir who had posted extra guards at the parliament. While he would not give my safety as the reason, such was generally assumed. The furtive glances of the guards in my direction as I passed them didn't lesson my apprehension. Each carried a Kalashnikov automatic rifle. I had no control over any venue in Kuwait, and my vulnerability was evident to all. The news media found reasons to photograph me on many occasions—all of which served to keep my face and odd position in front of those whose attention I would like to have avoided. Those who would attack me, or those who would like to see it done, surrounded me. "My soul is in the midst of lions; I lie down amid fiery beasts–the children of man, whose teeth are spears and arrows, whose tongues are sharp swords" (Psalm 57:4). My mother's psalms were beside me as I walked through this morass.

By early May, parliament was beginning to wind down with the onset of the summer heat, and my own anxiety over the wedding rose. After all, I did not really know Tahara. She was a Christian, beautiful, and bright, but I had not seen her now for weeks. Arrangements for the wedding celebration had taken off, and Hibah was in charge. She saw no need to consult me. I was ok with that. The cost of the wedding was 250,000 Kuwaiti dinars (about 800,000 US dollars). Although it was customary for the husband to pay for the celebration, the fabulously wealthy Al-Thani family assumed most of the expense. Their emir could not afford the possibility of an inconspicuous wedding. He needn't have worried about that.

When the date arrived our family boarded the short flight to Doha, and were greeted by a pack of reporters from local news agencies and Al Jazeera. There were few questions and many photos. If there were questions, I had no answers. The wedding celebration on the evening following our arrival took place near the beach in large tents: one for the women and one for the men. The men consumed several sheep, and the poor roasted creatures, surrounded by grilled green vegetables and tomatoes, stared up at me from their silver funeral pyres. As the husband, I was expected to eat an eye, which I did. The consistency was a mixture of fiber and gelatin, and the taste was salty. By this time, I could have eaten a frog.

The *Ardha,* also known as the dance of the swords, went on what seemed like forever. Lines of traditionally white robed men moved back and forth toward and then away from each other all the while brandishing their swords in mock combat. Part of the performance featured a thrust up and down of the swords. The sexual metaphor was clear. As much as I wanted to avoid participation in the spectacle, I was forced to emulate the flashing strokes with the steel blades. I hoped the others were more certain of their skill than I.

The Qatari emir made a brief but spectacular appearance. His summer dishdasha was whiter than all the others. *How had he achieved this?*

A white spotlight followed him about the tent. He greeted me warmly with kisses, stayed about an hour, and departed with his armada of Mercedes. We could hear the music from the tent of the women. When I was finally taken to Tahara whom I had not yet seen, she was adorned with the traditional henna and a brocaded gown that exceeded reason.

Then, finally, at 3 a.m. we were alone.

The next afternoon we flew south on Qatar Airways Flight 678 to the Seychelles where we stayed at the Ocean Jewels on Praslin Island. We were both struck by the isolation of the splendor we saw there. I couldn't grasp why God could create such beauty, only to allow it be swallowed up by the warming, rising sea.

Neither could I apprehend why God would provide this remarkable woman for me. We were scheduled to be here two weeks, and in this time we got to know each other wonderfully well. Our bedroom opened to the sea with no opportunity for others to invade the view, either of the sea or us.

But even here the tide of events in the Gulf intruded, and I was forced to face the fact that there was more to come. It was surely by design that a man who identified himself as Anand Kulabali phoned our room on the third day of our stay. We both listened on the speaker phone. Friends in Qatar had informed him of our visit, or so he said. Tahara said, "Oh, you live here in the Seychelles." He did not respond.

We asked if he knew Fareed, and he replied, "I am aware of Fareed." Anand welcomed us to the Seychelles and asked to meet us for lunch. We saw no reason to decline the polite invitation, but why had he been notified of our visit and what was his purpose? And why was he contacting us on our honeymoon? That was very strange. Even so, we were both curious, and felt protected by distance from problems in the Gulf.

Kulabali, perhaps twenty-five years old, was younger than we expected. His hair was thinly cropped, and he had no beard. His caramel-colored skin, chiseled jaw and high cheek bones left us uncertain of his racial origins. We met him in the hotel lobby, and he shook my hand, but not Tahara's even though she extended it. He smiled but didn't give his reason for the invitation. He had secured a private room off the main dining room for our lunch.

"I know you're wondering about this meeting. I think you will find this side room is the safest, most secure place for our discussion. I'm here to represent a group of men from Kuwait and Qatar who have great interest in the events occurring in the Gulf."

Tahara interjected, "There are many events occurring in the Gulf. To which do you refer?"

"I speak of the rise of Christianity in the Gulf. You know the numbers are much higher than the news media portrays. You must think now that I am a Christian. I'm not. I'm Muslim, but the group I represent thinks there are distinct advantages to the present course of events, and that we may secure an alliance. I'm Shia, a Twelver Shia." So this was the reason he declined to shake hands with Tahara. He went on with the standard Shia story. I closed my ears for a moment, but I couldn't shut out his refrain. "We are the oppressed Muslims of the world. You see this throughout the Muslim world—in Iraq, Syria, the Gulf, and North Africa. The nature of the oppression we experience is multifaceted, rooted in the past, but confirmed and solidified by current political and economic forces. My brothers in Bahrain and throughout the Gulf cry out for solutions, for resolution of the injustices inflicted upon us." Even more dramatic word choices followed.

I needed to know where we were headed, "We're very aware of the plight of your people. We sympathize because we experience the same thing, but what does this have to do with us?"

"I know about the silly reconciliation conference in Doha in

February. The roadblocks you saw were expected. You yourself anticipated them. In addition to the economic and political factors, the theological differences are clear. We emphasize the coming end of time when the last Mahdi and Isa, or as some call him, Jesus, will come and free us from our earthly chains. We have nothing else to look forward to." He drew his chair closer to us and spoke in a low voice.

"You may wonder now about me personally. My father was from South Africa and my mother is Indian—from Delhi. I was sent to school in Bahrain where I first experienced the subjugation of my people. There I became a member of "The People of the Return"—as we are called in English. We look to the end of time with relish because we will triumph only then." The People of the Return? That term had no clear definition to me.

"But what about us, the Christians?" asked Tahara.

"You are the People of the Book. We believe you will be taken to safety with us by Isa."

Tahara, her face warmly glowing toward the man, and apparently grasping the subtleties better than I, continued, "We want you with us, but you can't come without knowing Isa. You must know that Isa saves only by His grace. There is no other way."

"Yes, yes. I've heard that many times. *In shā' Allāh*, or as some say, as God wills." Kulabali glanced down at his napkin.

Tahara would not let go of this important concept. "But it's not at the *whim* of God over what we do. His grace is bestowed *as a specific plan.* He chooses you, and then you must choose Him."

"I've trudged over this ground before—it's as God wills." It was clear we were not going to convert him at lunch. He continued, "All I want to accomplish today is for you to know there is a group of Muslims, a significant group, who are with you. Now you know the name of our group. You will hear it again. Please enjoy the rest of your lunch." With that he was gone. He hadn't touched his chilled jumbo shrimp, and Tahara took them for her plate.

Tahara and I were alone the remainder of our time in the Seychelles. Enjoying one another in the sea and in our room by the sea. The water was far clearer than my view of the future. We wondered now even more what the Lord had in store for us. Tahara's faith in the future exceeded mine by a great measure. I couldn't conceal all my questions about where we were headed. Hibah had filled her in on my wandering, sometimes delinquent spirit before the wedding, but Tahara was kind, patient, and trusting in God's will. I was thankful to Jesus for that.

We did not see Kulabali again during our honeymoon, and we wondered where the Shia issue would lead. We knew the Shias were a small, but still significant, group in Qatar and Kuwait, indeed all over the Gulf, but we were at a loss to guess what they could actually accomplish in \societies dominated by the Sunni community. Would they ignite in others the fire we saw in the eyes of Kulabali?

But first there were the changes that would occur with the new family structure. We headed back to Kuwait where we would join Papa and Hibah in our old Ahmadi home.

CHAPTER 4

TWO FAMILIES NOW

Tahara and I had not decided where we would make our permanent home, and the Kulabali visitation had only added to that uncertainty. *What were we anticipating? What was I searching for in this morass of information that had assaulted me?*

The marriage meant we were in for changes, but events moved so fast I couldn't keep up with them. As we arrived at the airport in Kuwait, Hibah met us. She was less enthusiastic than I expected: polite but serious. She hugged Tahara but I noticed that she kept her eyes wide-open. She looked at me, and I could almost hear her saying, *so you're moving in with me, eh?*

Yes, Hibah, I'm afraid we are, and I wish you didn't look so serious.

We left the airport parking lot and drove to Ahmadi, and what was now a large family compound with plenty of physical space for us. The unspoken plan was to see how all the players, mainly the women, fit together. What effect would the addition of Tahara have on the mix? As beautiful and loving as Tahara was, she was also a woman of uncompromising vision and ideas. I had learned this about her during our honeymoon. Right away I saw the ground shaking between the two women. The tension in the car was something even a man could feel, and I was at a loss as to how to prevent any conflict. Hibah had made all this happen, but now, it seemed, she was afraid there would be clashes. The only choice was to move forward.

My father had added a wing to the home just south of the garden, and we put it to use. There we could be to ourselves, but still be part of the family. We had an entry into the courtyard, and the swimming pool construction was underway. My father said, "We need to give the women some distance." I think he knew we were in for problems. The distance was twenty meters and the physical barrier was a high, cinder block wall covered with light brown stucco.

But the physical barrier was not nearly enough. The women involved in the new grouping were vibrant, vital, and assertive, and the cinder blocks were no obstruction to their interaction. And then there was Divina, who had raised Hibah. My father and I looked on, waiting to see what would happen next.

The blend of Tahara, Hibah, and Divina turned out to be more volatile than I imagined. The morning of the first breakfast together was a harbinger of what lay ahead. The orange juice was frozen, not fresh-squeezed. Tahara had been accustomed to the best all her life, servants for every menial task, and the juice wasn't adequate. She said nothing, but all of us saw her expression when she tasted it. I was upset with her for this silent complaint, and voiced my displeasure later. My involvement was no help and converted a small issue into a big one. She didn't speak to me the rest of the morning.

Only the fact they were sisters in Christ prevented a complete breakdown of communication. The tension was not over any principle, but rather who would be the chief of the household. As the newcomer, Tahara was not the choice of either Hibah or Divina. Hibah had been the one to plan the marriage, but she had not intended Tahara's invasion. Remarkably, Hibah had not thought it through. Neither had we, and the two of us were still reeling from the Kulabali encounter and questions about our future course.

The next day Tahara said, "We'll have fish for dinner. I'll pick up the hamour at the market down by the sea."

Hibah responded, "Definitely not. I've been planning a nice fresh leg of lamb for a week. We can't just change plans on a whim." Divina stared coldly at Tahara. *Why did we care about the choice of flesh to eat anyway?*

Tahara answered, "I wasn't consulted about the lamb." I was shocked the relationship had sunk to the level of fish versus lamb so quickly. I left the kitchen as fast as I could. I should have stayed but I wanted no more of the matter. I was a coward when it came to any emotions—particularly those of women.

Two months into our stay, Tahara spoke to me about Hibah, "We've got to get your sister married." My father and I looked at each other, as helpless as two men could be.

Tahara proposed the solution. "I'm phoning my brother, Fareed. He needs a wife. He's older than Hibah but, never mind, I think it will work." Would such a move would lead us further down the path already exposed by Fareed and Kulabali?

I consulted with my father, and he said, "I'm out of this one. I'm too old for this." He wanted any excuse to avoid the conflict, but soon he sat down with Hibah and assumed his fatherly role, which he had mostly abandoned. I listened through the screen near the porch as they sat in the garden by the white mustard plant my mother had cultivated. "Hibah, we must talk about a marriage for you." I saw how uneasy my father was. He didn't look as happy as one would expect of a father proposing a match.

"What marriage? I don't have a suitor."

My father continued, "It has been proposed to me that Tahara's brother is suitable and desirous of a wife. He's never been married."

"So that woman wants me out of here. Papa, I don't want to leave." Hibah's eyes were wet, but she didn't cry openly.

"I know how you must feel, but you're nearing forty." *How could he know how she felt?* As for me, I felt responsible for my sister's sadness. She was being sent away. My father and I had given into the awkward arrangement and allowed the conflict to develop under our noses. We were both ashamed we had permitted it to get to this level.

"Papa, I have a life here now. I'm in demand as an attorney. I'm good at it, and Christians are being helped. I don't want to leave. I'm helping the believers here."

"Her brother Fareed is coming for a visit. See what you think. I've not promised anything."

And so arrangements for the visit proceeded. Hibah was hurt, but as the days went by she accepted the apparent solution. She spoke little with the rest of us for a week, but then her demeanor brightened again, the semblance of our mother announcing itself in her countenance.

Hibah and Fareed met under awkward conditions. Fareed was well-spoken and nearly an intellectual match for Hibah, but he was balding and overweight. He looked and dressed more European than Gulf Arab. His appearance did not overwhelm, and he had done nothing to make himself look better. Their greetings were stiff and formal. They shook hands and nodded, smiling politely. Fareed was past the day when he could be a convincing suitor. Hibah avoided seeming eager. Their first meeting closed after they both told of their commitment as Christians.

There was no doubt about the purpose of the visit, and each knew what was expected of them. There was no good reason for either to reject the match, and both realized it was time. The custom of the Arab world would prevail. There would be a period of getting to know one another after the agreement from each to proceed. Still, there was a pall over the whole thing, a feeling that they were driven by necessity.

Neither was opposed on principle. Hibah said, "I understand the marriage idea seems good. He is indeed appealing to me from a practical point of view but we don't know each other. I need more time." She had already seen beyond Fareed's physical appearance and into his heart, which was set on Jesus. I knew the issue was resolved, but we couldn't say so yet.

Fareed understood more time was required and took an apartment in the Hawali area of Kuwait so that the two could meet several times a week. Hawali was a busy, somewhat lower class section of Kuwait City with small shops selling cheaper goods, coffee shops, and fast food restaurants of both Western and Eastern variations. The streets were lively at night, providing a noisy, impersonal place for the two to go for a walk. From there it was a short drive down to the sea by the city center near the two towers. The seashore with its evening breeze was known as a place for young people in love to go for a stroll.

Fareed and Hibah were not in the category of young lovers, but they knew their purpose. They did not have an immediate physical attraction, which had occurred between Tahara and me, but the time they had together was satisfactory to both Fareed and Hibah. The time passed quickly, and after two months both agreed the match was acceptable. The date was set for October 2022.

As Christians they could not obtain the marriage license contract through the Qatari system in the usual manner for Muslims. Again, the Qatari emir intervened, just as he had for Tahara and me. The state representative knew he would be replaced if he failed to issue the document. Ultimate control of the state had its privileges. The wedding arrangements mirrored our own with similar costs. Some of the joy of our own marriage was lacking, but the arrangements proceeded smoothly as the pattern had been set.

Fareed and Hibah thus settled in Qatar, where Hibah was given a royal dispensation to continue her law practice with a Qatari license. Of course, there were Qatari believers who needed her help just as the Kuwaitis had. Hibah agreed with the arrangements for her new life. "Yusef, I know God has brought me here for a reason. I wait with expectation. Fareed is a fine man, and in time I'll learn to love him." The joyous emotion that accompanied a new marriage was not present for either. My sadness in imposing this on my sister kept coming to my mind. I don't think anything had hurt me as much since being in Evin Prison.

Divina moved to Qatar with Hibah. My father and I regretted her departure. It must have been awful for my father, knowing Divina had been his deceased wife, Rabea's, best friend and confidant. But for Divina, Hibah had replaced Rabea. My father thus had to give up Divina *and* Hibah.

Tahara and I were alone with my father, and the household settled into its old routines. The respite was brief.

CHAPTER 5

THE SHIA ARISE

The family conflict paled in comparison to events taking shape with the Shia, first in Kuwait and then in Qatar. Were these the actions Kulabali predicted? What might they have to do with my role? I had no idea.

First, it began quietly, and if we had not been alert to the possibility, we would not have noticed. The Burgan Bank came under assault by Shia members of its board of directors. There were accusations of mismanagement made against the bank president who was a Sunni. The report circulated that he had directed loans preferentially to Sunni borrowers rather than Shia families. Most knew this procedure was a common ploy throughout the Gulf. The overall purpose was to secure the financial resources of the countries in the hands of the Sunnis to an even greater degree than was already the case. The papers were reluctant to report on the internal bank conflict, but the rumors of it spread in Kuwait and then in other Gulf States. Soon the directing of bank funds to Sunnis became widely known, even though the media was afraid to disclose the practice.

Shia members in the Kuwait Parliament introduced a bill that a monitoring committee be appointed by the emir to watch over the lending practices of all banks in Kuwait. The outcry from the banks was remarkable in its vehemence. The quote from the *Kuwait Times* read in part: "that the government would be put in the position to look over the shoulder of private institutions is an abomination to investors."

The *Arab Times* took up the challenge with an editorial, which stated: "Kuwait is a country on the edge of democracy. For the government to interfere in the financial practices of private institutions is an insult to the intelligence, and even the rights of the Kuwaiti people." An Internet blog appeared shortly thereafter, which revealed that the editorial author had been paid off by a group of wealthy Kuwaitis who were, of course, Sunni.

I was singled out by Shia supporters of the bill and asked to give my support. I had expected a hiatus from the fray due to my recent marriage, but the bill was considered a routine part of my parliamentary status. What could I do to avoid this? Perhaps a well-chosen sick day?

Tahara said, "You've been put in this position for a purpose, and you don't look sick to me!" I pulled myself together and got on with it.

My speech to the parliament was simple: "Fellow Parliamentarians, let us not be at an impasse over such a mundane issue. Of course, we must promote equality among all Muslims, whether Sunni or Shia. All of us agree on that here. The Quran tells us so. The only question then is how to achieve this. If the present situation requires we monitor the lending practices of our financial institutions, then we must do so in a manner as unobtrusive as possible. The present bill achieves this aim. The bill carries no penalties, only the oversight and requirement that the findings be reported to the emir. I urge its passage." With this speech, I felt I had fulfilled my duty. There were more occasions for me to speak, but I avoided them. When other members challenged me, I folded my hands on the desk in front of me and smiled at them.

The measure passed by a bare margin. Would the result fall into my lap?

I should not have been startled by a request to come and see the emir. "Yusef, I thank you for your wise advice to the parliament. All I want here is the peace of Kuwait. I have confidence you're the one to bring this about." I knew he had picked me because he didn't care if I took the blame. "I want you to choose four men to work with you on the committee to investigate the lending practices of the banks. You will not be able to look at every loan; therefore you must be selective. I chose you because of your charisma and your skill in financial management and negotiation. Most of the banks mean well, but there are others who are determined to breed dissent. There is this Esau Allison; you must know of him. He was dismissed from the Ahl-Ali Bank, and as you may recall, and we had him deported for his awful crimes against our country." *How could I ever forget this? Once again, we were challenged by the tricks of my estranged half-brother.*

"But there have been requests by prominent citizens for his return, and I have chosen to agree with them, and do this as quietly as possible. Of course, everything's political. He has done favors for many in positions of prominence." *This was all unbelievable. Never had Kuwait seen such treasonous debauchery.* I remembered the photos of Esau's forced departure. *How could he be forgiven, and with no charges set against him? How could the collective memory be so brief?* "And now he's back, this time on the board of directors of Burgan Bank. You must watch out for him. I've heard he bears ill will toward you. He behaves irrationally." *Then, Your Highness, why did you allow him back?* I nearly asked out loud. The emir was his old political self. Every move, every act, was thought out, considering all the alternatives.

I thought I was rid of Esau. How foolish.

I picked four men from the parliament for the committee: two Sunni and two Shia. The two Sunni, Al-Bader and Al-Ghanaim, were among the richest men in Kuwait. The two Shia were men of modest means. I assigned the two Sunni and two Shia to review individual bank loans of the past year during two-day periods of each month at all of the banks. There would not be sufficient time to investigate all loans, which was never our intent. Given that there were twelve banking institutions in Kuwait, the task was accomplished in two months. Remarkably, the task was completed in ten of the banks with almost none of the infighting that would normally have characterized such a task in Kuwait.

In two of the banks, however, we were not received so graciously. At the Burgan Bank, the chief financial officer placed us in an isolated room with the air conditioning turned so high that we shivered through the review. When we tried to leave to use the toilet, we found the door was locked from the outside. We were released from the area only at five o'clock, whereupon we made a dash for the restroom. At the Gulf Bank, we were given the requested information and escorted outside to the smoking area at the rear of the bank. There we were occupied with the review while holding down the papers in the stiff breeze.

Both institutions were found to be abusive in the area of loan allocation. The Gulf Bank had given Shia clients only one loan in the past six months, and the Burgan Bank none. The information was reported to the emir as directed by the bill, and the emir chose to handle the information by himself. Afterward, he made a brief speech, in which he reported proudly, "The great majority of banks in Kuwait deal justly with loans." The two, who were not deemed just, were singled out by the emir as not respecting the qualities of fairness typical of Kuwait. But the emir was calming in his demeanor. He continued, "I'm sure these two institutions will correct their policies." I could not imagine that the problem had been settled with so little contention, and the two banks did not comment on the emir's statement. The fact that we had not uncovered more bank indiscretions was attributed to the likelihood that the other banks had had the time to cover their tracks. I puzzled at the mildness of the report and its soothing effect. Tahara reminded me again that the Lord was in charge.

But the Shia controversy was not over. The apparently favorable resolution of the banking bias only empowered the Shia, and inflamed the Sunni who claimed they had been disenfranchised.

I was amazed to find that this comparatively well-off group of Kuwaitis, the Sunnis, would go to the trouble of causing difficulty for themselves and others, especially in the financial arena where they already had ultimate control.

As Tahara and I dined at Mais Alghanim, the Lebanese restaurant down by the Gulf, a group of men gathered in front and began chanting. The date was Friday, July 28, 2023. We were on the second floor of the restaurant and could see the incident unfold. First, ten men with green headbands and without shirts gathered in front of the restaurant. The fact they were bare-chested was an affront to propriety. Then, twenty more joined them. The second group brought a green flag with the Shia *shahada* emblazoned on it: "There is no God but God, Mohammed is the Prophet of God, and Ali is the Friend of God." They began chanting while bowing forward at the waist in time with the phrasing of the words. The show continued without interruption for fifteen minutes and showed no signs of stopping. It was peaceful, but distracting.

The restaurant manager was irked that his business might be damaged, so he summoned the police who arrived quickly. They attempted to quiet the men peaceably; this approach failed and more police were called. Finally, the demonstrators were arrested and taken away in white vans without windows. By this time, one of the TV stations had a camera crew on site. They focused their cameras on the areas where the protesters were most concentrated.

Later that evening, the news exaggerated the event as a "violent" demonstration. The anchor said, "Earlier this evening we witnessed a "revolt" of Shia citizens at a popular local restaurant.

At Mais Alghanim, fifty Shia revolutionaries threatened to attack patrons in the restaurant. They were repelled and captured by Kuwaiti police."

As Tahara and I left the restaurant, one of the other guests accosted me with, "This is your fault for defending the Shia in parliament." In fact, as far as I was concerned, I had done nothing. I was uncertain about what I could or should do.

The newspapers did not deal with the Shia in a forgiving manner and neither did the justice system. The *Arab Times* reported the incident, and their description was not at all like the actual event. "Our reporters have learned that more than a hundred Shia mercenaries attempted to overrun the restaurant, Mais Alghanim. Many of the combatants possessed long swords with which they threatened police. While the Shia claimed their actions were a demonstration against bias perpetuated against them, several finally admitted they were present for criminal action. Five of the men were identified as Iranian." We heard the police had liberally used torture to obtain the required admissions. The typical method of the Kuwaiti police was thrashing the soles of the prisoners' feet, a remarkably painful and effective method. Those so tortured would be unable to bear their own weight for days.

The men were tried quickly in the Court of First Instance, and the penalty levied was based on the charge of insurrection. They were convicted, given prison sentences of five years each, and sent to the Central Prison on Sulaibiya Road.

The root of the Kuwaiti overreaction was actually its fear of

Iran. This dread had been building for many years, particularly with the concern over Iran's development of nuclear weapons. Additionally, Iran continued to assist the Iraqis in their attempts to restore their borders to what they deemed the historical location. Consequently, the Iraqi-Shia influence, it was feared, would invade from the north into our country.

The reaction among the Shia community was surprising in its speed and ferocity. A social group we had scarcely heard from quickly became vocal and apparent. Each Friday for several months, Shia families joined together and marched respectfully down several main thoroughfares. On the Fahaheel Expressway one Wednesday morning, the marchers blocked commuters which resulted in traffic jams and intense honking. The sight of nearly a hundred black-robed women holding their children by their hands and leading them down the roadway was startling to those proceeding to their jobs. There were violent gesticulations by both sides, but no show of physical force. Kuwaitis are, in the main, peace-loving.

In front of Mubarak Hospital, the entry area for visitors was impassible because of the crusading Shia.

Several Shi'ite faculty members at the university released the text of a study showing that the economic capacity of each Shi'ite family in Kuwait was overall less than half that of a Sunni family. They read their paper at a conference of visiting economists at the Sheraton Hotel. The attendees from outside Kuwait displayed expressions of outrage. "May Allah have mercy and may He shower down his wrath on the rich of Kuwait." Most of the sympathizers were from Gulf States with similar, Sunni-favoring economies.

The emir summoned me to his home to discuss the uprising. I was becoming more familiar with the palace than I wished. When I arrived there were no other officials present, and I was ushered into his presence by a single servant. I still didn't have an idea of the direction of events nor of my role in them.

"Yusef, I want you to take on the responsibility of evaluating the actions of the Shi'ites. I'm concerned there is more behind them than simply economic and political causes. I've studied their theology, and I find their motivation and practice to be significantly different from mainline Islam." He was correct on that point.

By mainline Islam, he meant Sunni Islam. We were alone in the room with its golden columns. The opulence of the setting conferred the true meaning behind his remarks. It was as if he had just said, *Let's keep all this for ourselves.* He continued. "I want to know where their theology is leading and what we should do to combat it. I have come to you because you're a Christian. The others (the Sunnis) have a built-in bias which impedes their judgment. I have no specific goals for you and no time line; I just want you to study the possibilities in an objective manner. And finally, you will report to me and no one else." *Report on what, really?*

"Yes, Your Highness, I understand and I will do my best. I see its importance." My desire was to get away from him as soon as possible.

As I left, he said, "Yusef, I will ask you to come to me periodically." Upon my departure, I noted that the grounds of the palace were otherwise deserted. Clearly, the emir did not wish our discussion to be known. The daily automatic watering of the lavish gardens was in progress.

I had hoped my exposure to the Shi'ite issue was closed with the conclusion of the pointless Sunni-Shia reconciliation conference in Qatar. Now, the responsibility for actually understanding Shi'ite theology (along with their social and political complaints) had been handed off to me by the emir. This responsibility was now mine alone, or so it seemed. Could I look to God for His assistance? "O God, do not keep silence; do not hold your peace or be still, O God! (Psalm 83:1). How should I approach this?

I first went to my refuge, the main library at Kuwait University. Given the almost total transition to electronic sources, its book section was deserted. I inquired about the location of Shi'ite theology books, and the librarian at the desk answered without even looking up from her computer. The designated area looked as though it had never been visited. The books were too well-ordered, none out of place. The volumes I sought were decaying with yellow pages, and the dust stifled my breathing. My Internet research had turned up two basic, old texts. The books I sought were copies of volumes dating from the second to the seventh century of Islam, the *E'teqādātal-Emāmīya* (or *Creeds of Shia)* by Shaykh Saduq and the *Tashih al-I'tiqad* by Shaykh Mufid. Their language was archaic and difficult for me to transfer into a modern line of thought. I spent three hours choking on the grimy texts and decided to abandon delving into the distant, documentary past.

More useful was a modern volume, *Fundamentals of Islamic*

Thought by Morteza Motahhari. At least this text was in modern Arabic and the line of presentation was linear. Even so, the subject matter was lifeless to me, and at six o'clock, the librarian found me asleep in the Shia cave, shook my shoulder, and told me it was time to go. By this time, a sandstorm had visited. The sky turned a dull red, and a new coating of sand covered my jeep. I felt I had made little progress in my attempt at understanding the Shia and Shi'ism. The day was a day of dust.

The next morning, I was awakened by a call on my cell phone from a number I did not recognize. It was Kulabali. He didn't identify himself, saying only as a greeting, "It has come."

"This is Yusef. Is this Kulabali?" I had no idea what he was talking about.

"You should have expected my call. It's happening sooner than we thought. The news from Kuwait has come to us here in the islands." His voice was high-pitched.

My response was less excited than his. "There was an event here at a local restaurant involving the Shia. We were there at the time. It was much less impressive than the news suggested. I think you may be premature." I hoped his timing was hasty.

"I know about all the events in Kuwait, but I am referring to your engagement in the process by the emir."

I asked, "How did you know of my conversation with the emir?"

"You must be patient, but you will soon know more. I want to know how you're coming on your assignment."

"I'm trying to understand Shia Islam, but the reading has not been not productive."

Kulabali replied, "It would take years to understand by reading. Perhaps you should enter one of the religious schools in Qom." He laughed emphatically. *Thanks, Kulabali. Qom was one of the primary centers of religious education in Iran, and no place for me.* "That's the reason I called. I have someone for you to contact. He's an imam in Kuwait. He's expecting your call."

He hung up.

Tahara was jubilant. "Now we're making progress. You must phone him right away." How could she be so elated about an upcoming audience with a Shi'ite cleric?

Two days later I summoned the mettle to call, and Imam Ali Khatami invited me to his home. I arrived at his modest two-bedroom apartment at seven in the evening. There were no servants, and his young son ushered me into the small study. I was not introduced to his wife. As Khatami entered, the son brought us tea and Oreo cookies. Khatami was dressed in a below-the-ankle black robe bound at the waist and his head in a black turban. His full beard was black and curly. He welcomed me with an easy smile.

"Well, Yusef, I've heard much about you and your family. I admire your father."

He was in no hurry, and he chatted about family matters for thirty minutes. I did not feel comfortable pushing him to the point. Finally, he said, "So, let's begin. My young friend, Kulabali, told me about your meeting. I understand you've been asked to play a part in our struggle. Now that the emir has asked you to report to him, this is a good time to proceed."

"But the emir told me my assignment was confidential. He's powerful and very careful. How did that information leak out?" If I was to be involved in some kind of *struggle*—how was I to be engaged?

Khatami responded simply, "He wished it to be known among some. My new friend, I understand you need to know about us. Don't waste your time with the old texts. You must listen to me. I am quite enjoyable to listen to." He was correct. His manner enthralled me. "We must meet many times."

"Imam Ali, I don't know where to begin. I'm not even certain why I'm here."

"There's no beginning and no end. We'll just talk, or rather I'll talk. Although we both read the Holy Quran, we, Shi'ites, differ completely from the Sunnis. They are the people of today. We are the people of yesterday and tomorrow. We look to the past, derive faith from it, and wait. I will be basic. Please pardon any reiteration, if it is such for you.

"The date of the Mais Alghanaim event was the tenth of the month of Muharram, July 28 on the Gregorian calendar. By that date and the occurrence, you should know that what you witnessed was Ashura." *How strange that not one media source had mentioned this fact.* "You must know Ashura."

I replied, "I've heard of Ashura, but I've never seen it celebrated before. I know it commemorates the martyrdom of Hussein, the grandson of the Prophet, at Karbala."

"Perhaps you know more than most Sunni Kuwaitis, if they care to know at all, but it's not a celebration. It is, as you might say, a remembrance of martyrdom. Just to say this, however, is incomplete. We look to the past, the sacrifice of Hussein, because it is the promise of the future. The Sunnis have only today, no past and no future. As a Christian, you understand this better than a Sunni."

Khatami called his son and asked for more cookies and tea. He motioned for me to follow him into the garden where the flowers were bright in color and fragrance. For a moment I thought of my mother's garden and the childish altar I had foolishly built to myself there, but I could not claim the same refuge here in Khatami's garden.

Khatami spoke again as we sat on a stone bench with the cookies between us. He ate more than I, first the white filling and then the chocolate cookie. Was this not the international standard? "There is another thing for our conversations. I'm embarrassed about this, but for the purpose of your understanding, I want you to call me *Sayyid*. You might say this is a term of respect. As a man I don't deserve respect. I sin. But Sayyid is a special term, indicating I am in the lineage of the Prophet."

Just then a bee-eater with a yellow throat and green back and tail settled on a branch near us. The bird's song was high-pitched, beautiful beyond comparison, and comprised of only three notes.

Sayyid continued. "You hear the beautiful creature God made. He has no voice other than what God gives him, for his voice he deserves no respect—only our benefit and enjoyment. So it is with me when I speak of things of the spirit. As a descendent of the Prophet and one recognized as possessing such a song of truth, you must consider what I share as special revelation." He stopped and looked directly at me for a time. "Yusef, I see from your expression that you're skeptical and not accepting of my position. Whether you accept or not, you must consider me a sayyid. As a man, I am humbled by the term, but, as a sayyid, I am compelled."

I felt the warmth and candor of the man. I sensed that whatever passed between us would be counted as between friends. I replied, "Sayyid, I understand."

The evening passed quickly. He knew I needed time to absorb what he had said, but the fact remained I had not integrated it into God's picture. I asked for the Lord's help in understanding, but little came to my mind. Perhaps my own arrogance was an impediment. I had not laid all my requests before the Lord. I felt as though I had more requests than I could put forth.

That night I had a dream. I was in a field of weeds. There was no grass, only thick-stemmed weeds with prickly points on the leaves. I tried to lie down in the field but could not because of the prickles, and I longed to escape from the field. Then, a group of horsemen dressed in green rode toward me and swept me up in their strong arms. I was taken to a place with no weeds, but only prison cells with steel bars. They left me there with no water. I awakened sweaty and thirsty. Tahara brought me a cold drink when I awakened.

I texted Sayyid. *Would you mind if I bring my wife to our next meeting?*

He responded. *No problem, but please ask her to be covered and not offer to shake hands.* Tahara dressed more conservatively than I had ever seen her do before. Her dress was ankle-length and her blouse was long-sleeved and gray. I was afraid she would revert to her Al Jazeera reporter mode and ask questions assertively. To some extent she did, but Khatami was gentle and tolerant. His backdrop of an extensive library lent authority.

She began, "I've heard about a white horse during Ashura."

"Yes, there may be a white horse and, if so, there would be no rider. The absent rider is Hussein, and the empty saddle symbolizes his martyrdom. The image is used to evoke the reality of Hussein's sacrificial death. The white, of course, is the color of purity. The riderless horse enhances the emotion of the participants. We say, 'A single tear shed for Hussein washes away a hundred sins.' Young woman, I see your troubled expression."

Her countenance moderated. "Sayyid, please forgive me for any impertinence, but you know we believe the tears of a man can't wash away sin."

Khatami continued, "I know what you believe, but you do not yet understand where the discussion will go. The tears for Hussein possess a transcendent value that is not inherent in Hussein or in the one who sheds the tears. I will try to peel away the layers for you and your husband. For the Shi'ite, truth comes in progressive deposits of verity that are revealed only as God allows, and they are revealed through the inspired imam as he interprets the Quran."

Khatami saw Tahara recoil from that portion of the discussion. She did not press the issue of the layers further. He spent the remainder of the time restoring and securing the relationship. He brought his young son in to meet us. The little boy, Khalid, was more polite and deferring than most Kuwaiti children his age. I was amazed at Khatami's personal skill.

Tahara and I left the apartment after another thirty minutes, got into our black Mercedes, and pulled on to the Fourth Ring Road. After a few quiet moments, Tahara said, "You know what he's saying is blasphemy. If I were a Sunni, I would say Khatami is a blasphemer. He is saying the Quran is not the final word, that an enlightened individual can reveal further truth, at least a further, deeper understanding of the Quran. It's like a Christian saying he can reveal further truth outside the Bible."

"Perhaps we should break off contact with Khatami," I responded, maybe cruelly. I was tired of the ongoing religious confusion, and what it did to me. Then, I softened my tone. "There could be danger if this is all exposed as the main contrast between Sunni and Shia. I suppose such thinking is well known to those who really care. We sure don't want to make things worse, but for now there is safety in keeping the discussion quiet. Kuwait has a long tradition of tolerating problems if they aren't debated."

Tahara was stiff with tight, thin lips. Then she said, "You know we can't stop. God has called us to this."

I wondered how she could know His calling when I was still wondering.

The next morning a white Escalade pulled up to our home in Ahmadi, and a tall man in a white dishdasha got out and rang the bell at the front gate. The guard in our courtyard took a white envelope from the man and delivered it to me. It was from the emir with his seal embossed on the envelope. It said in part, "I need your report on the Shia situation within two weeks. The state of affairs has become critical."

My conversations with Khatami took on an accelerated character. I informed him of the urgency imposed by the emir, but he was not troubled by the potential danger that might be behind the emir's request. He responded, "At last, we're moving toward a conclusion. The Shias are a people of faith. You must understand this."

"But faith in what?"

He gave no direct answer to my question, but continued. "The essence of our belief, or for that matter any belief, is faith, not works. I see that shocks you. We are a people of repentance, a repentance that is emblematic in Ashura. Hussein represents for us a moral and spiritual victory in the face of tyranny. His death epitomizes a collective atonement, much as you would say about the atonement of Christ. Hussein's sacrifice went beyond the historicity of the event. It was an intervention of divinity that provided promise for the future. As an imam it is my duty to expose the truth for those who don't know it. The layers of truth in the Quran are to be revealed."

"Even if the truth goes beyond the Quran and hadith?"

He replied, "Yes, even if it seems to go beyond, especially if it goes beyond. But of course, the levels of meaning hidden in the Quran hold all. They may require the imam's spiritual insight to discover them."

As I departed that afternoon, I was followed. The vehicle was a red Toyota Tacoma pickup with no license plate. The truck had been parked a block away with two men inside. They pulled away from the curb and followed me as I left Khatami's apartment. I didn't tell Tahara. "O my God, I cry by day, but you do not answer, and by night, but I find no rest" (Psalm 22:2). That night, I slept fitfully at best.

When I returned to Khatami's home for the next visit, I noted the same small red truck had followed me. I thought Khatami should be aware of the potential danger, so I informed him.

He replied, "What did you expect? Danger always precedes great reward. As I've said, we look to the return of the last Mahdi who is the twelfth imam. He has been in hiding for more than 1000 years, but he will return to signal the end of time and a reign of justice, perfect divine justice. Then Isa will return, and time will conclude. We are the People of the Return. Let us proceed."

We sat in his small book-lined study with the Oreo cookies he loved. We both could see the red truck parked in the street a block away from the apartment.

He continued. "I shall turn to the political aspects. This is the heart of the emir's concern. Do you think he's asking you for theological wisdom? Surely, you don't believe that. The Kuwaiti Sunnis aren't yet much troubled by us because they don't think about religion, not in any serious sense. If they began to think about us, when they begin to think about us, they will hate us." He got quiet for a minute and looked up the street at the red truck.

"We reject Sunni authority because they distribute power based on the fickle thought of the religious gentry, their so-called *ulamas*. These are the self-appointed spiritual leaders of their day, not chosen by God. Their power comes from what they refer to as *consensus* of the community or the *umma*. They're only a continuation of the tribal consortium that preceded Mohammed. They are no different than the Umayyad dynasty that ruled our ancestors by political fiat. It's a failed attempt at rationality because it is a human attempt. We deny the authority of the political leaders of this day." So much for that piece.

I responded, "What you're saying may be treasonous." Tahara had already identified the religious ideas as blasphemous. How much worse could it get? And must I follow this course in defiance of the rulers in charge?

Khatami went on, "Let me lay out the political picture for you. You're already aware of the components, but let me put them together. We deny the authority of Sunni leadership. It's as plain as that. It's not just that we differ in our mode of prayer. As you may have observed, we pray with our hands at our sides while the Sunni pray with hands clasped." He mimicked the Sunni prayer posture. "But there's more, much more than our visible stance before Allah. The difference is *in the heart*."

"The politically important fact is that we consider the rule of Sunnis to be tyrannical. Their laws do not define our piety. We reject Sunni nationalism. Their theology, Wahhabism and Salafism, counts only the Quran in its barest form, devoid of wise spiritual interpretation. We go beyond that, and seek to know all its layers of meanings." *Again the layers.* "Wahhabism and Salafism typify the thinking of the Saudis and ISIL and all the other so-called fundamentalists. We reject all this. We are with the Shia of Iran and Iraq. Yusef, we are on the verge of war. And even though we are the minority, the promise of the return is the promise of ultimate victory."

At every visit with Khatami, my concern rose higher. What struggle had I been pushed into this time? I was not at all where I wished to be. "Do not hide your face from me in the day of my distress! Incline your ear to me; answer me speedily in the day when I call! For my days pass away like smoke, and my bones burn like a furnace" (Psalm 102:2-3). Would my days disappear, not only from my control, but from my life too? This day passed without a satisfactory answer.

It was time to make my report to the emir. I was summoned to his executive headquarters near the Dasman Palace. The building's tan minaret dominated the approach. I asked to make the report verbally and not in writing; in this anonymity, I sought some kind of protection, but the request was pointless. A tiny little spectacled scribe was present to write down my every word. His feet didn't reach the floor from his chair.

I spoke for perhaps two hours. I was not served tea. At the end the emir dismissed me without rising as would have been customary. He did not speak to me but only to the scribe. He said, "It's worse than I feared."

Binyamin came to see me the next morning in Ahmadi.

"Why didn't you just phone?"

"It's too important, and they may be monitoring our calls. I'm picking up communications that concern me. Their content is encrypted and I haven't yet broken their code, but I can see the senders and recipients. That's my concern. The connections are novel and they all have Esau at their center." *Esau—back in the picture.* "Both ISIL and the Persians are carrying on dialogs with Esau as the intermediary. The Iranian messages originate from an organization with the letters MEAF. I can't figure out why ISIL would be in contact with Iran. I believe the messages are referring to Saudi Arabia, but the Saudis are not participants.

MEAF likely stood for the Persian Ministry of Economic Affairs and Finance. Was the originator of the messages my old chief Khadim, the one I had served in order to receive a reprieve from Evin prison? There was no other source I could think of with those initials. And Khadim was still the boss. I was upset over the information. I thought I had left all that behind.

CHAPTER 6

FOR A TIME, I DESCEND

Then my dreams collapsed in upon me again. Lately I had not been harried by my dreams. Since my marriage I had only had that one about the prickly grass. I guess I thought I had escaped the dream attacks my father had also experienced, that perhaps this hereditary condition called narcolepsy had somehow ceased. Surely, my Christian heritage and good behavior sheltered me, such that I could avoid the dark cloud of dream invasion. But no.

The news of MEAF and Khadim hammered my daytime consciousness with the old fear that I might be dragged into the morass that was Iran again. I feared I couldn't escape the penalties that still lurked there for me. Surely, my forced participation in obtaining nuclear weapons for them would not be forgotten. This prospect dashed me into a depression from which not even Tahara could extricate me.

The dreams began irregularly, and I failed to see them as a pattern at first, but it was not long before I recognized the fact that the troubling visions occurred after I was already awake, yet unable to move, which only doubled my dread. Initially, the visions began from the recollections my father had conveyed to me about his life. First, that fearful, demonic white camel, and then all the rest. He had confessed all he had done before he was converted to Christianity. I suppose he thought it might protect me to know, but the sins of the father, and I knew this all too well, are visited on the sons. The Old Testament leaves no doubt there.

The awful recounting of my father's disasters invaded my mind, as if I had committed the same acts myself. There was the vision of the dead child lying on the pavement and the broken bicycle at the curb; the death of the child had been covered by a blood money payoff to the child's destitute parents. Then there was the proposed abortion of his illegitimate child during college days, the torture of his affair with Sattie, his professor, and then his cowardly desertion of my mother, Rabea, during the Iraqi invasion. Why did his sins attack me?

Oddly enough, the most fearful specter of my father's visions was the white camel who entered at critical intervals. I knew from my father's tales how damaging the phantom animal could be. Then, as quickly as they had assaulted me, the visions of my father's life ceased.

Instead, visions of my own life overcame me. My sojourn in Evin prison visited me with all its constant dread and doubt. When the dream continued, it seemed to never end. Would I ever be released? Even though I was free in Kuwait, the sense of imprisonment was with me as fresh as the days when I was there. Would I suffer amputation of a hand? How would the verdict come down? And then there was the bomb guilt I carried. How had I made such an awful contribution to the Iranian war arsenal? Could I ever escape this? And now the possibility that I might be asked to return to Tehran loomed. Would I see Evin prison again from the inside?

When the visions invaded, Tahara had to abandon our bed. She couldn't stand seeing me sweating, not moving but with such expressions of pain and fear. She didn't criticize. There was too much about me she still didn't understand.

After two weeks, God intervened. I recalled one of the psalms tattooed on my soul by my mother. "Like a dream when one awakes, O Lord, when you rouse yourself, you despise them as phantoms" (Psalm 73:20). Suddenly I was able to despise these dream periods for what they were.

CHAPTER 7

THE QATARI SHIA

For the next two weeks, our lives in Kuwait assumed an uneventful pace. The dreams were over. The wealth of our family no longer required any actual work to maintain our status, and I attempted to fill my days with minor parliamentary items, enjoying Tahara, and our regular worship in my father's growing church. Because of my rank and position, or so I thought, the church had been allowed to grow without governmental intervention.

If there was a mission for me in the future, I wanted to avoid it.

Several members of the church invited us to their beach cottage at Nuwaseeb near the Saudi border. The drive down to Nuwaseeb was always entertaining: the wealth of rich beach houses on the left side of the road going south, and the herds of camels, goats, and sheep crossing the road, each in turn.

We took the turnoff from the main road toward the beach. The *dhubs*, spiny tailed lizards, some nearly a meter in length, scurried in front of the car and into their burrows. Their population had long since recovered after the Iraqis had eaten most of them during their invasion.

The church families were not restricted by Muslim dress customs, and the time near the ocean, while still modest, was more Western in character. I learned Tahara couldn't swim. She was so accomplished in other areas that any departure from competency surprised me, but the gently sloping beach allowed wading far out into the warm water.

There was a sandy shoal two hundred meters from the beach, and I swam out with two other men. In the shoulder deep water, we talked for an hour before swimming back. I think Tahara was peeved that I left her for so long. We were still newlyweds.

We barbecued the fresh-caught faskar or seabream on the beach along with fresh vegetables on the grill, and the men and women ate together. The evening turned to night, and the stars brightened, first Venus in the west. For a time, we were disengaged from the lights and news of the city. My mother's psalms sought me. "When I look at your heavens…the moon and the stars…what is man that you are mindful of him?" (Psalm 8:3-4a).

But the respite was short-lived, and the Shia issue took a new turn. Because of our late return back to Ahmadi, we slept late. At 7:30 the next morning, my cell phone woke us. Hibah was on the line, and she sounded frightened. "Can you hear the sounds in the street just outside our home? You've got to come down to Doha right away. Please hurry. You may be able to intervene." *Me? Intervene?* I was still trying to determine the direction I should pursue.

She startled me into alertness. "What's wrong? Yes, I can hear the noise. It sounds like shouting and explosions."

Hibah, said, "It's been building here for some time. We thought it would pass. The emir has been on top of it and saying he would punish violence. Emir Tamim has met the Shia's complaints and actions with strength, but now it's turned to fighting. The Shias have directed their demonstrations to areas near the royal family. Fareed thinks that's why they're here. He says they won't hurt us, but I'm afraid. The smell of the burning tires is awful. We're stuck in the house."

"What can I do?"

"I don't know yet, but I've learned the Shia here respect you. You must have said things or been helpful at the conference."

"I don't think I did or said anything, but of course I'll come."

Tahara insisted on going to Doha with me. We packed one suitcase each and headed to the Kuwait airport. We checked the television system in the crowded main corridor of the terminal and located the earliest flight to Doha. Flight 347 on Qatar Airways boarded in forty minutes, no time to relax in the first class lounge. Upon arrival in Doha we rented a blue Chevrolet Impala and proceeded to the home of Fareed and Hibah on the Pearl, but the police had blocked the bridge.

I rang Hibah who picked up her cell immediately. "Yusef, they've had to block off the island in an attempt to keep the violence from spreading. The Shia concentrated their rioting to the Pearl because it's a wealthy area. The police won't let you cross."

We took a room at the Royal Riviera Doha and paused, but we had no idea what awaited us. Here we were in a luxury hotel while the fighting in the street spread. How typical of the Gulf. That evening our room phone rang, and the Qatari emir's secretary stated I should come to the Emiri Diwan Palace on the bay at eight in the morning.

A new Cadillac Escalade picked me up the next morning and drove rapidly to the palace. The vehicle seemed heavier than usual, and the doors were weighty. I was taken to a small room off the main hallway. The walls were hung with light blue, thick drapes, and the floor was gray Italian marble. There waiting was Emir Sheikh Tamim, along with Hussein Al-Husseini, the Shia whom I had met at the reconciliation conference. I was embarrassed to be the last present. The servant brought the usual tea and disappeared, slamming the door behind him in disrespect. The emir scoffed, "Another Shia in my house. From this moment on, he'll feed his children by sweeping the streets."

The emir opened, "Thank you very much for coming so quickly."

I broke protocol and interrupted, "I'm worried about my sister, Hibah. I came to Doha to make sure she's OK, and now I can't even get to her."

"Never mind. I have a contingent of soldiers surrounding their home."

Now, I was even more concerned. Soldiers, not police, were required for their safety.

The emir continued. "We have a most serious situation here. I'm afraid it's gotten ahead of us. The Shias, mainly the poorer ones, have put together what might be called a revolt. However, none of us are to repeat that word outside this room. For now, we are calling it a civil disturbance, but frankly we must combat it as a revolt." He looked to Al Husseini.

He took up the explanation, "Yusef, I'm glad you've come. You were helpful during the conference in preserving moderation." *Once again, I thought I had contributed little.* "The conflict in progress, the civil disturbance, is becoming widespread. At first we thought we could confine it to the Pearl, but we've failed. To answer the question you must have, *no*, it's not religious. It's mainly social and economic at this point." He hesitated for a moment and took a deep breath. His hands were trembling. "The situation has occurred among the poorest of the Shia faith, and has spread upward. Once it takes on a political structure it may never end. And the religious component, well, that's another thing altogether. The disturbance is springing up in at least ten sections of the city. Most of them are in the poor areas."

I realized at that moment that Husseini's motivation was to protect the status quo, mainly for his own family. This eruption in Qatar made the Shia-Sunni conflict in Kuwait seem adolescent in comparison. It was my turn, "Why have you asked me to come this morning?"

The emir began again, "Yusef, you're in a unique position. First, you're from a respected family, and you yourself are well thought of both here and in Kuwait, because of your ordeal in Iran." Apparently I was still deemed a hero for being a prisoner. "Because you're known to be a Christian, you have no bias in the Sunni-Shia controversy. I had attempted to conceal your faith, but now it's an advantage to us. And finally, you've married into my family. And there is another reason we'll discuss later. But I have an initial request to make of you: I want you to assist us with possible negotiations."

I immediately recognized that the emir's use of the word *request* was a euphemism. He pressed a button under his gilded chair, and within a moment the double doors opened and the servant brought in two Shia imams who wore the standard black garb. They nodded but didn't smile or offer the usual polite Arab greetings.

"Yusef, these two gentlemen represent those who are protesting against my government. I want them to explain their case before us. I present Imam Baraghani and Imam Mokri." Both names were Iranian.

Baraghani began without making eye contact with the emir or making even the most basic deferential gestures, and proceeded thus, "We are here today because we have been summoned. We do not consider ourselves prisoners, but perhaps we are. We know we are not under the rule of law. We are ruled by the monarchy, a monarchy that defies the constitution that was approved twenty years ago." These were fire-breathing Shia patriots. "We know our religious beliefs are not the issue. The issue has been economic control, and now it is control by the power of the state over us as Shia. We're done with peace; it has been taken from us."

I perceived this was the time for me to enter the discussion. "Honored sirs, I am not from Qatar. I am not Sunni or Shia. But

I have been called here. What can I do to calm your concerns?"

This time it was Mokri who spoke, "You must free us from our subjugation to these people. We ask for the same justice afforded the Sunni. We will not tolerate less, or it will be civil war."

The emir was becoming infuriated, and he did not conceal it. "I have asked you here as men of honor, but you threaten civil war. You do not even possess the means to carry out your threat. The Shia in the streets will be crushed." He pressed the button under his chair again, this time three times in rapid succession. The door opened and six soldiers with AK-47s appeared. "Take these men into custody. We will charge them later. They are, by their own admission, guilty of insurrection."

The emir then turned to me. "Yusef, I must apologize for bringing you here to see this. I see we're beyond dealing with this on a rational basis."

I had to speak: "I see the depth of the problem, but my personal concern is the safety of my sister and her husband."

He replied, "Yes, we will assist. We'll see they're taken to safety."

I was shown out of the room and down to the same armored vehicle, but this time there were two similar vehicles, one in front and the other in back. We rushed off toward the Pearl.

We arrived at the roundabout just before the four-lane road to the Pearl. The road was barricaded, but we were allowed to pass through with the addition of a military jeep leading the way for our entourage. When we arrived at their home by the sea, Fareed and Hibah came out to the line of four vehicles. Divina was there, too, crying, standing behind Hibah. All three were dressed in sweatshirts and sweatpants. Hibah's hair was not covered, and the lines in her face pointed down, and she wore no eye makeup. Their bags were already near the curb.

As we left the Pearl by a different route, there were signs that a battle had occurred. There were wrecked vehicles, some with bloodied bodies still in them. I couldn't be sure whether they were government soldiers or protestors. Three- to four-foot craters were scattered throughout the roadways, indicating that one or both sides had used more than small arms. We drove north on Highway 1 until we reached Al Shamal, where we left the main road and arrived at the emir's vacation house on the beach. A three-feet thick concrete wall topped with razor wire surrounded the two-story, white building. A large swimming pool and fountain stood between the house and the sea. Shortly after we arrived, an armored vehicle arrived with a contingent of twenty soldiers who stationed themselves outside the wall.

The Qatari emir rang my cell phone. "I'm confident you and your family will be safe now. I'm afraid I brought you to Qatar too late for our internal negotiations. We'll have to get through this and then we'll talk about the other reason for your presence." The *other reason* hung in my mind. Why didn't the Lord make it clear to me? "Be not deaf to me, lest, if you be silent to me, I become like those who go down to the pit" (Psalm 28:1). God had gotten my attention, but I heard no answers.

For the Qatari emir, the next few months did not go well. The civil disorder was quelled only with force. The display of arms necessary to bring about quiet was appalling, even to the well-to do Sunni. Any sense of moral superiority was shaken. The constitution, approved by national vote in 2003, but never implemented, finally had to be applied in order to restore some degree of order. All the citizenry knew its application was just for show. The emir, who had been quite popular, saw his status shrink to a pitifully low point. The news company started by the ruling family itself, Al Jazeera, became a tool in the hands of potential reformers. Only by surrendering considerable power was the Qatari emir able to maintain a semblance of the old order. The other rulers throughout the Gulf were aghast and disgusted. If the power of one of them had been diminished, it affected the power of all. The earlier collapse of the Qatari relationship with the other Gulf countries, particularly the UAE, Bahrain, and Saudi Arabia, also contributed to the hovering conflict, and the fact that Saudi Arabia was at the heart of the Gulf state disruption only heightened the concern among all the participants. What was Saudi Arabia's game in this anyway?

By the time order was restored, Tahara and I had returned to Ahmadi, where I had two years left in my parliamentary term. I knew I had done nothing, but I still appeared in the news with regularity, perhaps because I had become a novelty.

In late January 2024, the emir's secretary told me to come to the palace. Once more I was taken into one of the smaller rooms. I greeted the emir with the necessary bowing and kiss. He did not smile or make sustained eye contact. I was not sure whether his demeanor reflected his concern over the situation or his dissatisfaction with me.

"Yusef, when you made your abortive trip to Qatar, Emir Tamim referred to a second need for your assistance. Now, it's time for you to know of this. We know Iran is behind the Shia revolt, both the one here in Kuwait that is presently small, and also the dangerous, destructive one in Qatar. You must go to Iran as my envoy—really the envoy of both myself and Tamim. Our consultative efforts in Iran have been ineffective and we can't get past the first level. We suspect they have a nuclear bomb."

I knew they had the device, since I had provided it. I also knew for certain that I could not return to Iran. Even though I was officially released from prison, I felt I had escaped. I couldn't face that again, and I told the emir I couldn't go back.

He replied, "Yusef, you must. Allah, praise be to His name, has chosen you for this day." So this was the choice of the Muslim Allah. "You're familiar with their governmental structure. You speak Farsi. You're not Sunni. Even though they put you in prison, they respect your abilities. That's what my informants tell me. I'm not sure why, but they feel you've made real contributions to their country, and, of course, you will go as my official legate. They dare not harm you."

The emir would not want to know of my contributions to Iran. He would not learn that from me.

"But what can I do? Do you really think discussion is going to solve anything?"

"You will go to Tehran. We've secured a flat for you close to the Ministry of Foreign Affairs near Pardis City. You must find out how they're getting support to the Shia in the Gulf. That's your main mission. This assignment will work under the shadow of your covering work, which is to discuss moderating plans with the Shia community." *So I was to be a spy. So much for peace talks.* "The Iranians have approved this single reason for your visit. They know only that your trip is for peace. Of course, they consider it a waste of time, but they're willing to tolerate this one purpose, to moderate the discussions with the Shia. The main purpose must be accomplished in secret."

How was I going to get the information the emir required? It was a mission filled with potential poison for me. Such was the cruel surprise just exposed to me. I had thought: *Surely I'll never return to that place again.*

Reluctantly I returned home to pack for Tehran, and try and explain to Tahara. This was not an encounter I hoped for.

As Tahara drove me to the airport, my cell signaled a text message from Imam Khatami. There were no words, just a photo of the red truck we had seen tracking us from time to time. I increased the size of the photo in an effort to see the driver. It was Afsin. I had not seen him since we had settled him and his family in Kuwait after their furtive arrival from Iran. I tried to convince myself it was someone else, someone besides Afsin, the young man I had relocated here as he fled from Iran for his Muslim sin of apostasy, the one who had sought Jesus as a child under my tutelage, surely not him. But no, it was really Afsin. *Why?*

CHAPTER 8

RETURN FOR IMPRISONMENT?

On arrival at Tehran's Imam Kohmeini International Airport, I withered from the memories of my disastrous return to Iran the last time when I had been imprisoned there. The airport interrogation of that day and subsequent trip to Kashan prison were as fresh as the day they happened. At any moment, I expected the approach of big-shouldered men dressed in black. As I passed through the Tehran immigration, the unsmiling expression of the attendant accentuated my recollections. The man in the military uniform and cap said, "*Bedrood*," which means goodbye. I was suspicious. This form of goodbye in Farsi was used only when a person never expected to see you again. Why didn't he say "welcome" or "hello" instead? I kept looking behind me, expecting a door to open revealing the security police. I practically ran out of the airport.

My anxiety rose without objective cause. I was there on official mission of the Kuwaiti government, and on a logical basis, there was nothing to fear. But I had followed the news accounts of the peculiar and unexpected measures imposed by the Iranian government on other visitors, and I imagined the same would happen to me. "Therefore my spirit faints within me; my heart within me is appalled" (Psalm 143:4). I was afraid I might really faint, and not just sense a weakening in my spirit. Before long, I emerged into the bright sunlight, and for a moment, my apprehension eased. A bearded young man got out of a dark blue Buick (an old one at that) with a sign bearing my name, and I was taken to my apartment near the Ministry of Culture and Islamic Guidance.

I kept checking my ankle for the confinement bracelet that was not present. I couldn't dispense with the need to escape.

The same silent man picked me up the next morning, and delivered me to the ministry's front door. He knew I was aware where to go from my past experiences in Tehran, and did not bother to show me. I found Conference Room 303 on the third floor, and the discussion commenced.

Three imams dressed in the usual black garb filed into the conference room. The table was about fifteen feet long inlaid with gold strips and blue iridescent gems. The imams seated themselves together at one end of the table with me at the opposite end. They made every effort to appear as severe as possible and never offered their names.

The one in the middle spoke without any customary greeting. "We are here only at the request of the Ayatollah. We know you speak Farsi, and we will therefore address you in our language. First, you should know we are *mujtahids*. To refresh your memory, this means we are the authorities in all matters relating to

Islamic law." I needed no such refreshment. "Our statements in this area are not subject to question. You are here to discuss a path to accommodating Shia theology with respect to Sunni theology. We are here to inform you that no such moderation is possible." This I knew too well. "Our system of authority is from Allah, all praise be to his name, and designated through imams. This authority cannot be questioned or delegated. You will discuss many things with some of our colleagues who are more eager to please. You will, of course, listen politely, but know our word is final. Are we clear?"

"Yes, you are clear. You must understand I'm here as a representative of the emir of Kuwait. You do not control the report I will make to him." I surprised myself with the courage I possessed to make such a statement, but there was no point in fear at this juncture.

The next three hours passed with more of the same. I sat quietly while the imams harangued. Lunch came with small sandwiches made with olives and avocados. The imams did not eat with me, but sat quietly with the food sitting before them as if to join me would be a sacrilege. They closed the meeting two hours after lunch. I was exhausted, and I wandered the busy streets for two more hours before returning to my quarters. The streets of Tehran were far more alive than the meeting had been.

I learned more from the streets than from the meeting too. The boulevards were crowded, and the stores displayed expensive goods—at least as stylish as Kuwait. The people were not only shopping, but also buying. The men were well-dressed in dark suits or leather jackets. The women, while still having covered hair, wore modest but expensive dresses and shoes. The shoppers were not at all restrained in their interaction between genders. Tehran did not present the picture of a closed society. For a time, my anxiety left, and I relaxed.

In the evening I went out again for a walk and ate a *shawarma* of thinly sliced and marinated lamb from a street vendor. As the sun descended, I walked through a local park with a lake where several mallards paddled. My day ended at a coffee shop near my apartment. No one joined me, but two men stood by, noting my lengthy visit. I felt like a spy.

We convened again the next morning in the same conference room. Breakfast of fried eggs and beef sausage with coffee was served to two clerics and me. They appeared to be of lesser rank than the imams of the previous day. One was Alireza Panahian, a middle-ranked Shia cleric and head of Ayatollah Khamenei's think tank for universities. The other was a very old man, Naser Makarem Shirazi. Shirazi was known for his denial of the Jewish holocaust and his release of a *fatwa*, a ruling on Islamic law, forbidding women from attending soccer games.

A scribe was seated quietly in the corner of the room. The imams of the previous day had not required a scribe. The young man recording the conversation did not look up from his computer keyboard, and even our greetings were recorded. That these two men were not trusted in their conversation, and required a scribe, reactivated my apprehension.

Shirazi began, "We have nothing to speak about. Everything has been decided. Nothing has been left to speculation. I know you are here to disrupt our theological position, but our stance is incorruptible. I did not study for so many years in Najaf and Qom to deal with a *kefer* (unbeliever). I am here only because the Supreme Leader commanded it." He did not touch his breakfast. I did not respond to his religious condemnation of me.

During Shirazi's rant, Panahian quickly consumed his breakfast. He looked up when Shirazi, exhausted from age and the exertion of his speech, settled into his chair. "Yusef, I want to thank you for coming. Of course, I agree with my illustrious colleague, but I know you're a man of peace here for the purpose of peace. We acknowledge that the prophet Isa will return at the end of time along with our Mahdi. So, I ask you to look to Isa whom you know."

What did he mean? I wished I possessed a certainty that God could save me from drowning in this conversational abyss. I was trapped by my own fear of my previous imprisonment, and the confounding doublespeak before me.

The two clerics played good cop/bad cop for the remainder of the day. Was this accidental or part of a careful plan? As we concluded and walked down the long hall of the ministry, Panahian touched my forearm to delay me. "I'm sorry for the long day and the frustrating discourse. You must know that we, as Shia, look to the end of time with expectation. We are the People of the Return. Perhaps you've heard that phrase before. We are as patient as the heron feeding in the shallows." Shirazi looked back, and

Panahian stopped for a moment as the old man was gathered by his attendant. Out of his hearing, he added, "Keep going to your coffee shop."

I avoided the coffee shop that night and tried to sleep. A dream intruded repeatedly, and I kept waking. In my dream I was held prisoner in Tehran again, and for an extended period. I attributed the dream to my unease on returning to Iran.

A series of similar meetings with clerics of lesser rank continued over the week. Their design was to convince me there was no ground for theological reconciliation. I got the point.

I returned to the coffee shop in the evenings. The small glass and metal tables were near the street, and I could observe young people hurrying by. The first of these nights I remained alone though I noticed that one young man passed me at least three times during the evening.

On the next evening, the same man approached and asked, "Can I buy you a coffee?" He was dressed in expensive blue jeans, Nike tennis shoes, and a Lakers T-shirt. *I wondered if he knew the Lakers had moved to Omaha.* He continued, "My friends tell me you're here to make peace between Sunni and Shia. Peace is an honorable mission, but you'll find it elusive."

He identified himself as Ali Behzadi and launched into the conversation and my confused thoughts with no hesitation. "Who do you think the last Mahdi is? That's the great mystery that's no longer a mystery. The Quran itself does not mention him, but the teachings of Mohammed make allusions to him. The key is Isa.

We know from your book that He will come again to fight against the false Messiah. You've heard of the Occultation, the idea of the hidden twelfth Imam. Yes? I have come to tell you this word is a falsity. The Mahdi has been hidden or made occult only for those who do not see. The Shia I represent see. We are *the People of the Return*."

I had heard the phrase from several sources and now it all came together. This phrase was being repeated to me, as if to deliver a message.

The crowd in the coffee shop began to clear out. Behzadi had positioned himself with his back to the security cameras, and I gradually moved my chair to a similar angle. I had long since been sick of their intrusive security measures. I responded, "I know there are Shia who emphasize the return of the Mahdi, but I have not yet heard the definitive characteristics of the one who returns."

He pulled on his beard and avoided the answer at first, "We aren't certain who he is or who he will be."

I said, "What if Isa is the Mahdi? Then, what will your view of Isa be?"

"Your question, I believe, is whether Isa is man or God. The proper answer for me as a Muslim is to say he is a man. I don't know, but there is no need in our eschatology for a Mahdi other than Isa."

I responded, "I was sent here to seek a common ground for Sunni and Shia, a reconciliation of sorts. You're taking me in the opposite direction."

"You understand the gravity of the situation. Please continue you visits to the coffee shop." And just like that, he was gone.

I went back to the four walls of my apartment, which, despite their adequacy, were assuming all the emotional characteristics of my former cell at Evin prison. I struggled out of bed each morning. The days continued in their repetitive messages from the imams thrown at me. They intended to tire me out with the standard litany, and they succeeded.

By evening I made my dutiful visits to the coffee shop. There, near the sidewalk, I was treated to a variety of young Persian men, all less than thirty years, who expressed thoughts similar to their first young colleague. They looked expectantly to the arrival of the Mahdi without knowledge of his identity or character. Thus, a repetitive message was hammered home.

I was informed that the daytime conferences with the imams of the *ulama* would continue for another week. Apparently, I had demonstrated a complete lack of understanding of their message. Perhaps these endless meetings were the meaning of my recurring dream of detention.

In the second week, the coffeehouse site changed. As I was sitting at my usual table, an older man passed and motioned for me to follow him. When I failed to do so, he rounded the block and tried again. This time I acquiesced, and we ended up in a small park overlooking a little lake facing the high mountains outside

Tehran. The lake's surface rippled and glittered in the remaining light. There was still a covering of white snow on the mountain crests. I could not see any security cameras in the park, and as the light waned, several street lamps provided the only illumination.

The risk for this man, Abu Ali Al-Evadi, was greater than for the others. He was the Christian pastor of one of Tehran's evangelical churches. For him to talk with me about the religious state of the Shia in Tehran would be a crime punishable by almost any sentence the particular court cared to impose. Abu Ali was a brave man, but he was cautious.

He knew my name. "Yusef, we will try to make you aware of what's happening in Iran and particularly in Tehran." I noted he used the pronoun *we*. "Since you were in Iran during your stay at Evin, much has happened. You had some taste of it in the prison, but there is much more now. The gospel has spread by the most peculiar means. We know your special area in this is dreams. There has been much awakening through dreams for individuals, but this mode of the Lord's methodology accounts for only a small number of conversions. Those who dreamed and then were exposed to the Scriptures told others, and then, well, you know how it goes."

Actually, I did not really know, but I sought God's answer through the pslam. "Do not hide your face from me in the day of my distress! Incline your ear to me; answer me speedily in the day when I call!" (Psalm 102:2). The Lord's responses were too big for me.

Abu Ali continued, "The conversions have been a great problem for the church. We have always been watched, but now they are more vigilant. As the size of our congregations grows, they have begun questioning new attenders. You know of the Basij. They are now a branch of the Revolutionary Guard. They're comprised of three brigades, and the all-female al-Zahra Brigade has been sent against us. They've forced the new converts to form underground churches. We attempt to assist and supervise the best we can, but the risk is great. Several of our group have been sent to Evin."

"Why are you telling me this? I'm happy for the spread of the gospel, but it does little for the Sunni-Shia question."

Three women, all covered in black, suddenly entered the park and walked purposefully in our direction.

Abu Ali said, "They're coming. We must leave." And he left by way of the unlit street.

The next evening the rain fell, preventing me from sitting by the sidewalk portion of the coffeehouse. A tall young man in blue jeans, a plaid shirt, blue jean jacket and tennis shoes approached me. His mannerisms suggested an approach for sexual purposes, and I initially avoided his gestures, but he whispered, "Abu Ali asked you to come."

This time the Basij did not follow us. How odd it was that Christian conversions were awarded higher priority for the Basij than homosexual activities. We took a taxi to Darband, where the hiking trail to Mount Tochal begins. As we ascended above the main city, the temperature fell. He stopped the taxi near a small, rocky stream that flowed down through the city from the mountain above. He took my hand as we walked together, which could be taken either as a normal gesture between male friends in the Middle East or suggestive of a sexual relationship. We continued under the cover of illicit sex, which was apparently considered less a threat than Jesus.

He began, "Abu Ali has been taken. He wanted you to know more than he was able to tell you. First, you must know I am Shia. I'm a member of the People of the Return. We are increasing our alliance with the church of Isa."

"What's the point? The reason must hinge on your view of Isa. I can't get an answer on that issue."

"You want me, a Shia Muslim, to tell you that Isa is Allah. I cannot do so. If that is the case, Allah will inform us soon enough. We have imams who will convey the truth. The Sunni do not. The important message for you is that the People of the Return are growing in number, and that there is no point of reconciliation with the Sunni." I was reaching the conclusion that the lack of reconciliation was for the best.

He let go of my hand and was gone. As he left he said, "You must go and smoke hookah." I did not know his name.

The daytime hours passed with a shuttle of imams of varying levels in and out of the conference room. The room with its teak-paneled walls and handsome conference table had become yet another place of confinement in my mind.

Later in the day I sought out a local hookah bar. A hookah pipe is an elongated glass tube connected to a glass base, which contains water. Flavored tobacco at the top of the tube is heated with charcoal, and the vaporized smoke passes down through the glass tube and into the water in the basin. The smoke is then cooled prior to inhalation though the flexible pipe held by the smoker. My family and I had always considered such smoking unpleasant, a lower class habit.

But I had followed my directions to this point, so I requested the pipe and sat on the thin carpet and lumpy pillow. For two hours, nauseated, I smoked and coughed alone. I wondered why I was there, but slowly the various conversations around me began to reach my consciousness. The smokers were from varied economic strata. Their sophistication of their dress and language betrayed them.

Two well-off smokers behind me with a dual outlet pipe went on about their work as professors at Islamic Azad University. The school has an estimated endowment of more than twenty billion dollars with outposts in other countries, including Great Britain.

One of the men, apparently an economics professor, said, "My classes have been audited by several representatives of the revolutionary guard. Thanks be to Allah that they don't understand what I'm teaching. They don't appreciate that our current system cannot be supported by our internal Persian economy. We're adopting international practices and they don't even see it."

The other responded, "I see the same phenomenon in my senior philosophy classes. Why do they come if they don't understand? I'm glad they don't grasp the ideas. Otherwise they'd see that what I'm teaching will lead to an overturn of the present system."

Over my other shoulder were three men who spoke as if uneducated. They were clearer in their expression. One said, "It's over for this country. I can't stand these cameras and the smelly little men who run around watching everything. If my wife wants to see a soccer game, it's OK with me." Two others joined in with like complaints having to do with infringements on their personal freedom.

I went back on several evenings. By the third day, the nausea had departed, and I was actually enjoying the smoke. By this time the theme was evident: the time was ripe for sweeping social and economic change. The great and heretofore unrecognized power and depth of this complex society was gaining a new maturity. I now had more to tell the emir than he would want to hear, but there would be even more complications.

CHAPTER 9

MONEY FOR THE REVOLT

The emir gave me a few more days in Tehran to wrap up the now insoluble issues of Shia-Sunni reconciliation. But more importantly, I needed to determine the funding sources for the Shia rebellion, which was the chief reason for my visit. I was desperate to complete my assignment and go home, but this question remained unanswered with no progress in sight. There was another source I had withheld until it was absolutely necessary. I phoned the office of Karim Khadim, my former boss, the head of the Ministry of Economic Affairs and Finance.

His secretary said, "Mr. Khadim does not see anyone unless he himself makes the request. Your personal needs are not the needs of the state." Nothing had changed with Kadim.

I went to the huge concrete-pillared edifice, designed to intimidate all who entered, and proceeded through the main door, which required passing through a metal detector and then a body search by hand. Finally, I located a directory on the back wall of the main hall. It was placed so it could not be easily found. Khadim's office was on the top floor, and the elevator to that floor required a key card entry. I waited for the elevator to open to others who were properly equipped, and entered with a confident nod to them.

After arriving at the top floor with two Brioni-suited, clean-shaven men, I stood behind a pillar and observed scheduled guests coming and going from Khadim's office. I tried to appear as if I were waiting for a colleague. Khadim's visitors went into his office, and each one looked anxious about their opportunity to see the great man. Finally, there was a lull in the flow of appointed guests, and the coffee-drinking secretary who controlled entry went to the bathroom.

I entered Khadim's office, and he looked up from his desk, which was large and inlaid with ivory. There were no papers or objects on the desk except for a large, leather and gold bound Quran. I doubted Khadim could lift such a tome by himself. Such was the true paraphernalia of power. The clean desk indicated others did his real work. He collected himself and said, "Yusef, I heard you were in Tehran. What are you doing here?" He didn't ask me to sit.

"I thought perhaps we could visit for a moment. Actually, I've come for information. I need to know how the Shias in the Gulf are being funded by Iran."

He broke into sustained, derisive laughter. "You've always had a thirst for knowledge. This sounds like the kind you get only from a dream. You should have no trouble with that." He laughed at his own joke. "Look, we know you're communicating with that rebel Shia, Imam Khatami. What are you plotting with him? You have no reason for seeing the man with such regularity." How did he know about Khatami? The red truck? Afsin?

I said, "I think you'll be happy to supply me with what I want to know." He reached toward the corner of his desk to press his panic button and summon his aides. "Don't press the button. When I explain, you'll be ready to assist." He settled back in his leather chair. "You recall the fortuitous sale of bonds we made to save your great country. We both remember how beneficial it was to your country, and I remember, too, how beneficial it was to you— that is, from the so-called residuals that were generated."

The color drained from his face, and his expression hardened. "You may think you recall but your recollection has no value. I am an honored man here. All in this building bow their heads and defer to me." He stiffened and marshaled his resolve. He was a proud man.

"I have more than my memory." I handed him a thumb drive. "Put the drive in your computer and look at the evidence. Again, there's no point pressing that button. I have another identical drive under my care at home in Kuwait."

The drive contained a record of all the bond transactions with dates of sale, amounts, and places of deposit. Khadim's one percent skim was documented with his personal bank account as the recipient. How could someone as smart as Khadim be so consistently trapped by his own actions?

"What do you want to know?" He put the thumb drive in his front desk drawer and softly closed it and locked the drawer with the key attached to his belt.

"We're confident the Shia in various states around the Gulf are receiving funds from Iran to support their disruptive activities. I want to know the details."

He picked up the phone and buzzed his secretary. "Cancel my appointments for the rest of the day." And then to me. "You've really done it now. We must leave."

I followed him with concern because I feared he might lead me into a trap. Once again my anxiety took the floor as I imagined being led back to Evin prison. We proceeded together out of the building through security, through the special door only for officials, and then to the car park, where he dismissed his driver and told me to get into his white Mercedes-Maybach S600.

The traffic police at intersections recognized his car and motioned us through the otherwise continuous traffic. We drove toward the mountains up into the high hills surrounding the city and got out near a grove of long-leaf pines. The cooling temperature did nothing to moderate the experience for me. I still expected a trap.

"I have long thought my office has listening devices I don't know about. They may also be in my car. Given what you have, I'll tell you what I know, which is considerable."

I was silent, waiting for him to speak and giving him no alternative but to tell me everything.

"We're transferring funds to your Shia friends at a rate of more than two billion dollars a month. I've been ordered to do so by the Supreme Leader. Given our current economic situation, we cannot afford this, but I have no choice. The money is transmitted to an offshore account in the Caymans where it's passed through an investment firm called Anaconda Derivatives who take ten percent of the funds. They're responsible for distributing the remaining funds as we direct. I ask you not to write down any of what I tell you. I know your memory is excellent. Please rely on it solely."

I put my pen and paper away.

"The Shia in Kuwait, Qatar, Bahrain, the UAE, and Oman each receive ten percent—that's fifty. Of the remaining fifty, twenty-five percent goes to the Shia in southern Iraq, and twenty-five percent goes to the Houthis in Yemen." I must have looked astonished at his last revelation. "Yes, the Houthis." I knew they were a group without adequate control or oversight.

Since at least 2014, Yemen had been a cauldron—quieter, less imposing, far less important than Iran, but still a boiling pot. They were too poor for anyone to care. The Houthi rebellion had ebbed and reemerged periodically, but the awful news from the failed state assumed the minimal and shrinking importance of all failed states.

However, as a Shia offshoot they were a constant worry to their adjoining northern neighbor, Saudi Arabia. Although the Saudis had attempted to punish the Houthis, they had succeeded only in solidifying the position of this strange group. The Saudi airstrikes had been shown killing children, making the Houthis' position more desperate and yet more heroic. And as usual, the United States was an accomplice, though mostly a silent partner, because they remained dependent on the friendship of the Saudis and the Saudi's support of Israel.

"I can't believe you're bothering with the Houthis. Are they really Shia?"

Khadim responded, "Yes, we must consider them so, for political reasons if nothing else. They're Zaidi Shias. They're *Fivers*, meaning they accept only the first five imams rather than the twelve. The theology here is irrelevant to their particular role. You should not wish to know their role."

We sat down, facing each other in the soft grass and cool evening.

"It is my purpose, my assignment from Emir Nawaf, to know. Remember, I have the proof needed to finish you."

He nodded affirmatively and went on, "There's a very specific reason we must continue to support the Houthis. We've given them the bomb. And remember you got the bomb for us through your clever business dealings." He did not need to remind me. How much longer would my sins plague me? I knew the Lord forgave me, but He had not relieved me of the consequences. But still this, this particular sin?

"That's insanity! The Houthis might do anything. Even the most sophisticated countries of the world can't manage nuclear weapons. The word *nuclear* just evokes madness."

"That's why we must continue to give them money, so they remain under our control. Right now, the Houthis have no idea what to do with the weapon; but when the time is right, we will show them, and we know whom to blame: your people, the Isa people." He shivered and pulled the collar of his sports jacket up around his neck. I was getting cold too. "The Houthis' threats to use it may be sufficient to accomplish our purpose. When the so-called great powers learn we have nuclear capability, thanks again to you, they will realize we won't use it. Whenever an established state gains the ability, they never use it. But they will be afraid of the Houthis, the ones who have no arbiter. The Houthis are to be the executor of our will."

We were both silent as we drove back down into the city. Khadim let me off at my apartment and said nothing. We both skipped the usual courtesies. The next morning, I flew back to Kuwait and tried to decide what to tell the emir. I cried out without praying. Is that possible? In such tears, there is no point. "Out of the depths I cry to you, O Lord! O Lord, hear my voice! Let your ears be attentive to the voice of my pleas for mercy! If you, O Lord, should mark iniquities, O Lord, who could stand? (Psalm 130:1-3). What about my record? Was it now a block to my communication with God?

When I arrived at the Kuwait airport and exited customs and immigration into the brilliantly lit, open waiting area where there were hundreds expecting arrivals, some with signs for those they did not know and others searching for their family and friends, Tahara was there alone. Her face was beaming, shining. She didn't

113

wait for me to speak: "I'm pregnant." Concerns about my burden faded for a moment, and we embraced more than the degree considered proper. She went on, "I can't wait to tell you about the baby and everything. It's due in seven months." She didn't know the gender yet.

In her ebullience, Tahara insisted on driving and talking, and the results of my investigative trip did not come up until later in the evening. What was so important a few hours ago faded for a time.

Finally, I said, "I must tell you about the trip. I have to report to the emir, but I'm not sure what to say. First, there is no chance of reconciliation between Sunni and Shia. We both knew this before I left. The emir must be made aware of how serious the conflict has become though, if he doesn't know already. Secondly, as we suspected, Iran is giving considerable money to the Shia around the Gulf and southern Iraq."

"There's no problem for us. It's not our business. Let them have at it." Nothing more important than a baby. What's the big deal about a religious war if you're pregnant?

"Tahara, there's more. They've given the Houthis a bomb." Tahara knew I was responsible for obtaining nuclear devices for Iran, but we had put that information out of our minds and consideration.

"Yusef, you can't be serious. They may want to set that bomb off in Mecca." Tahara had gone rapidly to the heart of the matter; and strangely enough, this had not occurred to me. "You can't tell the emir about the bomb. The trail might lead back to you." Her demeanor changed; our growing family was now threatened.

The next morning, as expected, the emir sent a car for me. He was anxious for my report. Of course, I would not tell him about the bomb. I wanted nothing to do with Yemen and the Houthis.

This time in the emir's personal quarters we were served a breakfast of unsalted white cheese, flatbread and apricot jam with tea and milk. The emir was bareheaded, and his bald head detracted from his kingly state. No others were present, no scribe. Apparently he wanted no chance for the information to be disseminated. He was not surprised there would be no Sunni-Shia reconciliation. The amount of money being transferred to the Shia did, however, surprise him. He was particularly astounded at the amount given to the Houthis. "Why is this little speck of Shiism given so much? Who even knows what the Houthis believe? I don't understand. You must find out what's going on with them."

"Your Highness, I don't know why they have been given such a large sum," I lied.

"Yusef, you've served me well. I need your astuteness to answer this question. I am making you my envoy to Yemen to meet with the Houthi delegation. You will also have to put up with Hadi's people too—at least in the beginning. You will leave in a week."

This was unbelievable. I never conceived such a punishment would come upon me. *There was nothing of God in this. If there was, I couldn't see it.*

On my way home, I called Tahara and told her the news. The cell made it possible for me not to inform her in person. I had never heard her cry, but she broke into tears. "I just know you won't come back."

I had go to Yemen? Surely, God had not chosen me for such a mission. He would not be so careless with His will. Avoidance was my only avenue. How could I avoid the emir's direction?

I had to confirm the source of Khadim's information about Khatami. *How had Khadim known so much about my comings and goings in Kuwait?* Afsin had not contacted me for many months, nor had he told me where he lived. Thanks to Binyamin's computer skills, I finally located his third floor apartment on Tunis Street in Hiwalli. I knocked on the door and his wife answered. She had covered her hair. Afsin came around the corner of the small dining room and saw me. "Yusef, no!" He knew immediately why I was there.

"Yes, I've come to find out why you're spying for Khadim." He looked at me and began to cry. It was like he was a child again in his father's home in Isfahan, afraid to tell me his dreams. "Why did you do this thing? Why betray me to Khadim?"

"We needed the money. I had no choice. I had to support my family." Now, his young wife was crying too.

I turned and went down the stairs. As fearful as I was of going to Yemen, and the certainty of my need to refuse the mission, the pain of his betrayal was worse. All I could think about was his supposed conversion to Jesus and the risks we had taken in getting him to Kuwait. Surely his dreams and new faith had been genuine. And now this. *What would become of Afsin? Was he lost or just weak? Why did he not come to me?*

And the greater question: *How could I avoid the emir's Yemen assignment?* Perhaps my resignation from parliament would suffice. *Or could I claim illness? Or just simply decline?* My father was still considered a coward by many for his desertion of his country and family during the Iraqi invasion. Perhaps a genetics excuse would succeed.

CHAPTER 10

YEMEN

None of my potential excuses eclipsed what appeared to be the Lord's plan. I couldn't refuse the mission, a mission God had set in front of me, one that I felt was the consequence of my sin in helping with the bomb. But God's plan took the day.

In late March 2024, with Tahara crying inconsolably at the airport, I departed for Sana'a, the capital of Yemen. The emir's ambassador in Yemen had secured my travel documents, which were scrutinized slowly and carefully by the Yemeni immigration desk personnel in the dark entry area. Those of us who were not Yemeni were relegated to the lesser personnel to the left side of the entry area. The Saudi and American bombs had done their damage. The airport, open irregularly, was in disrepair from the fighting and government disruption that had occurred over the preceding years.

Yemenis passed through quickly, while visitors like me were scrutinized thoroughly. Each foreigner was inspected as if he was a spy. This was possibly true. In the customs area, my bag was taken completely apart, and my old volume of Whitman's *Leaves of Grass*, passed down to me from my father, was confiscated. How did they know it contained traitorous material?

Two groups met me in the lobby, each competing for the upper hand. The first to reach me were the Houthis who informed me they were in charge of the visit. Next came representatives of the old Hadi government, who similarly informed me of their superior status. The Hadi representatives were on their last legs; actually they were mostly finished. The remnant of the Hadi government resided in Aden, with their leader, Abd-Rabbu Mansour Hadi, scurrying between the safety of Riyadh and medical treatment in the United States. I was surprised the Houthis had even allowed them to show up and greet me.

The two groups each brought up a vehicle to transport me and I was forced to make an awkward choice between them. The Hadi group headman whispered, "I'm sure you would prefer to be with us rather than that rabble. They don't even use cologne." I must have looked at him strangely.

The Houthi driver said, "It's better you go with the winners, not the losers." I had to agree with him. And because of the information I was seeking about the Iranian money transfer, I got in with the Houthis.

"*Ahlan!* (Welcome!)" came from several sitting in the vehicle.

Our vehicles proceeded together and we soon ascended a hill overlooking the city to the Mövenpick Hotel. As we drove up Berlin Street with me in the Houthi car, the passenger-less Mercedes and the three following vehicles that the Hadi government had sent followed closely behind us.

The hotel rests on a prominence with a commanding view of the city. The formerly spectacular outdoor swimming pool was nearly empty, and the remaining water was discolored from lack of use. Leaves and empty candy wrappers floated in the artificial swamp. I could see the minaret of the huge mosque built by the former president, Ali Abdullah Saleh, ostensibly to honor Allah, but really to honor himself. It had been untouched by the bombing. The Saudis had been careful about at least some of the mosques.

Neither the Houthis nor the remnant of the former Hadi government were aware of the reason for my visit, but the possibility of wooing the Kuwaitis and receiving financial incentive was their first consideration. Arguing between themselves, the two groups attempted to agree on a schedule for my time. I was courteous to both and endeavored to reassure them. "The emir has instructed me personally to survey all your needs."

My mind kept returning to the information given to me by Binyamin. Why the unlikely contacts between Iran and ISIL? How did the Houthis fit into that? I was still unconvinced the Persians would award prominence to either ISIL or the Houthis. And why was Esau in the middle?

The two groups proceeded with their own versions of the schedule. The Houthi representative in charge said, "First, we will see the old city and view what the Saudis have done to our beautiful country." We motored over the ragged roads, concrete rubble piled in the center, and into the old center of Sana'a to view the remnants of the formerly elegant, walled city. Many structures had been damaged in the bombing when the Saudis attempted to dislodge the Houthis, but the remaining square shaped buildings with their brown stone construction, and white-outlined windows of rectangular and arch shapes, almost random in placement, yielded a fairy-tale picture as if the facades were made of chocolate cake with white icing. The remaining minarets were the candles.

The two groups took me into one of the antique buildings, and we ascended a narrow staircase with steps of varying heights. We arrived at a dirty third floor apartment where a physician, who was no longer employed due to the destruction of his hospital, served us tea. "You can see I'm reduced to doing housework now that I can no longer go see my patients in the hospital." The doctor emphasized his newly acquired poverty. Their overall purpose in bringing me to this sad man was a demonstration of their despairing condition.

The competing delegations continued a gentle tug-of-war with my time. Each wanted to display their view of the country's undeniable need. I settled the competition by giving each group a single alternate day in the dilapidated city.

The Hadi group wore suits and ties of a style popular twenty years earlier. The Houthis sported the more traditional Yemeni tribesman garb with head covering, thob (a long robe), ragged sport coat over the robe, and the Yemeni *jambia* (or dagger) in the front of the chest mounted on a wide leather belt. I retained the Kuwaiti red and white gutra and white dishdasha.

Leaving Sana'a, our convoy proceeded south toward Thamar passing the remains of Thamar University, an impressive set of buildings that had sadly been destroyed by the Saudi bombing. We rapidly passed through a little town, oddly named al-Qaeda, all dust and filth, the outdoor markets still bustling.

After many hours we reached the seaside city of Aden where Abdullah from the Hadi urged me to confer with those there that had remained loyal to old government. He grabbed my arm and said, "You must meet with these men. They're expecting you, and it's a matter of honor for us to bring you to see them." I complied. The Houthis understood the honor issue and gave the day to Abdullah.

Among this collection the Hadi delegation had put together, half supported the unified Yemeni government under Hadi authority and half remained loyal to the idea of the two Yemen states that had existed prior to 1990. The representative of the newer government said of the men on the other side. "For this time we must sit with communists." They were more than uncomfortable meeting together, and I wondered if a fight might erupt, but there were only words—the typical fare among distant Arab brothers.

Aden was much more British in its orientation; the old city still retained the feeling of a British colony. The group representing the Hadi government were more polite, at least in the Western framework, than the other Arabs, perhaps a remnant of the British influence.

But the day and night were a loss. The competing internal elements of the Hadi group made any kind of progressive discussion impossible. We closed the day by going down to the sea for a swim. As the Hadi group was not the recipient of the funds for Iran, I was anxious to get on track with the Houthis.

Abdullah went on. "Out there in the harbor they bombed the U.S.S. Cole, and they disabled the big ship with only a raft." The others of the Hadi delegation nodded in agreement, proud of their countrymen's cleverness.

From that point on, I resolved to spend as much time with the Houthis as possible. I had to get rid of Abdullah and his Hadi group if there was to be any serious discussion with the Houthis, yet I was aware of the need to preserve their infernal honor. I gushed in thanking the Hadis for their attention, told them I had learned much from their beneficent care of me, and informed them that the remainder of my mission would concentrate on the Houthis. The Hadis looked at each other without smiling, keeping their heads slightly bowed. Several paled, perhaps from what their boss might say. They mounted their convoy of four vehicles and headed back to some site unknown to me.

That night I called Tahara from my room at the Gold Mohur Hotel on the beach. She was still crying, frightened about my continued presence in a land under self-siege and Saudi-siege. Tears were so uncharacteristic of her that I hoped they were simply related to the worries induced by her pregnancy. Then she said, "Your father has been taken to the hospital in Ahmadi. I don't think it's serious. He has a minor chest infection, but you know he's eighty-five."

"Should I come home now?"

"No, I'm just having morning sickness, and now your father's not well, but it does not seem serious. I'm OK. You must complete your assignment." Her courage had briefly reemerged.

The next morning the Houthis and I departed north for Taiz. The roads were in disrepair from years of irresponsible and unfunded government, and my chaperones were anxious to show me how much they needed an infusion of funds from the Kuwaiti government. They hit every bump. Clearly the money from Iran had not been spent on infrastructure.

We took several side roads up into the hills to smaller villages. These small towns on the steep hillsides still appeared as fortifications, a relic of the days when one tribe raided another. In their desperation, do they still? Women carried whatever firewood they could find scattered by the road and water from the few remaining wells. Small children of indeterminate ages played with stones as toys, their bellies protuberant, their skin pale, and their hair with a reddish cast. I could not decide if their hair color was due to the henna dye used as a cosmetic or malnutrition. I suspected the latter, and my caretakers were happy to emphasize the famine.

By this time, I had become acquainted with the chief of my hosts, Azziz. He cut a smart figure with his out-sized, jewel-handled jambia. He let me look at the weapon. It was dull and clearly for decorative purposes only.

He had been reared in the mountains around Taiz. He opened up to me as we drove: "Our country is on a broad highway to destruction. We don't know what to do to save ourselves, unless it is something that has potential to generate major attention to our needs." Was he referring to the nuclear weapon they reportedly possessed? He continued, "Our poverty is well-known. This has been stated in the press the world over to the extent that now, when our needs are mentioned, no one pays attention anymore. We're running out of water. Our children have no real food. We cannot govern ourselves. We have no system of education. I'm supposedly a leader of the Houthis, and only just this year have I learned to read."

At first I was sympathetic but then it occurred to me they were receiving nearly $500 million a month from the Iranians. Where were the funds being used? They could provide banquets for the starving children with that money. There was no evidence of it benefitting the population.

We arrived in Taiz late in the evening and took rooms at the Al Saeed Hotel overlooking the city from its commanding position on the mountain. The hotel had suffered from a long lack of tourists, and the rooms and halls were in need of paint. Only the first three floors were in use as the elevator no longer worked.

The next afternoon we proceeded to a local tearoom where fifteen men had gathered on the floor in an oblong oval. At intervals about the circle were piles of leaves called *qat*. Qat is a plant whose leaves contain cathinone, an amphetamine-like stimulant, which initially produces a state of euphoria and enhanced well-being. As a guest I was urged to participate in chewing the leaves. *No* was not an answer they would accept.

Those near me persisted in selecting the newest, most tender leaves and expected me to enjoy them. "Please, take some more. These leaves are the best." Soon all of us had a large ball of the leaves resting on one side of our mouth, tucked in our cheek. This telltale appearance was widespread in Yemen, and now I knew why. The use of the drug was epidemic among all classes.

While I felt little or no effect of the drug—other than the unpleasant presence of leaves in my mouth—my colleagues in the circle gradually began to speak more forcibly and with greater speed. They rattled on about trivial matters as if they were of prime importance.

"The qat is much better this year."

"Our soccer team could beat the Persians if they would play us."

On it went. I didn't know how to manipulate the leaves in order to achieve their maximum effect, and I had no desire to learn.

As the afternoon crept on, the state of exhilaration dissipated and was replaced by an overwhelming fog composed of cigarette smoke and the mental haze finally induced by the qat. All together I found the afternoon a completely unpleasant experience. That night, although I was famished, we skipped the meal. Qat suppresses the appetite for those accustomed to the drug.

The next morning, we struck out for Hodeidah on the Red Sea coast. Azziz was apologetic for the qat. "I know you were perturbed about the qat chew. None of us in Yemen can escape it. It's our way of life. Everyone chews, all levels: doctors, day laborers, teachers, women too. We know the cost, but we will not leave it. The crop requires much irrigation with the water we don't have for other uses."

I responded unkindly. "I know you're asking for Kuwaiti money. Should the Kuwaitis pay for your addictions?" All the while I thought of the great sums they were receiving from Iran. Who really benefitted from those funds?

They put me up in the Taj Aswan Hotel. From there we proceeded over to the unkempt beach for a swim in the Red Sea, which I found surprisingly cold. Then, a large group of Houthis joined us and we stopped at a seaside restaurant and sat under a large tent to be served. The meal with the fresh fish and shrimp was the best I had eaten in Yemen. We finished off the meal with *bint al-sahn* ("daughter of the pan"), a light, flaky pastry topped with sesame seeds and honey.

On the way back to the hotel, I was finally alone again with Azziz. I opened the essential conversation, "I know you're receiving large sums from Iran. I need to know what's happening to the money. My government will not give assistance unless this information is available to us. There is something going on here in Yemen I don't understand." Azziz fidgeted. "The money from Iran is so large that the sum alone could instigate a war, but I am seeing no benefit of that money here. Why is that? What is it being used for? The Hadi faction provides no opposition to you. Who is your enemy? The Saudis have stopped their bombing for the present. Is it the Saudis still?" The Americans had just pulled the plug on their support of the Saudi war.

"Our situation in Yemen is one of great complexity," he answered. When he heard I knew about the money, he removed the wad of qat leaves from his cheek and flung it into the trash. I wished I hadn't told him. "The friends we have today may not be our friends tomorrow. Therefore, we must act quickly and always the day before our comrades choose to abandon us. We've already been betrayed by some of our own. A small group has joined something called the People of the Return."

Again I was abandoned by the present and led into the future. I was confused by events. I didn't who my enemy was, though I was certain they were there. "Be gracious to me, O God, for man tramples on me; all day long an attacker oppresses me" (Psalm 56:1). I didn't know how prophetic this psalm actually was. Again, my mother was there with her psalms.

I continued with my mission, "But Azziz, the money, where does it go? Why is it not being used to help your people?"

I saw now that Azziz was exhausted in maintaining the subterfuge, so much so that he finally told me the truth. "We send the money directly to our friends in ISIL. Yusef, I know what you must think. You think I'm wrong, but I'm not. And I'm not making the decisions. It comes from on high. The Saudis are our enemies now, and ISIL is the enemy of the Saudis. Even though we are Shias, we've taken refuge with the Sunnis of ISIL against the Sunnis of Saudi Arabia. You already know the fragility of our position." He shrugged his shoulders and shook his head in dismay. "You should have been able to figure that out on your own. If you didn't understand it today, you would have by tomorrow. Now, you must give me you cell phone." He didn't verbally threaten but his hand rested on his jambia, even though I knew it was dull.

We arrived back at the hotel where Azziz left the Isuzu Trooper in the front car park. I followed him to the locked basement where the now large group of Houthis gathered. There were more than twenty young men mingling loudly. In the center of the room was a large metal box with several padlocked latches.

Why had the trouble coalesced in Hodeidah? This small town on the Red Sea was settled as a key distribution point for incoming goods including weapons and drugs and for the outgoing distribution of funds and non-electronic communications. The Houthis and ISIL had relearned the ageless value of verbal messages, which were not subject to modern monitoring techniques.

Several of the participants pulled the curtains on the upper level windows of the basement room. Our meeting was now private. The qat was already on the floor in proper positions, and the chew time began. Azziz sat next to me. My position was deteriorating from guest to captive, and my cell phone protruded from his belt.

The complexion of the gathering gradually changed. I noted packages of pills and powders being distributed among the group, and the Houthis eagerly grabbed for the prizes. The pills were swallowed in large quantities. The powder was consumed by several means: some was placed in hookah pipes, while some was scraped onto knife blades, heated, and the aroma inhaled.

I looked to Azziz for explanation. The pills were Captagon, a powerful manufactured amphetamine used by ISIL troops, and the powder was hashish.

The drugs had their effects. There would be no need for another meal tonight for these men. One by one they began to stand, unable to sit still. They moved without direction. Then, they began to shed their robes, leaving only their loose-fitting trousers. Their jambias landed in a pile in the center of the carpet around the metal box. Uncontrolled laughing began, and the men gestured to the container. Some made the verbal imitation of an explosion during their wild dance. Finally, I heard the cry from several, "Mecca *halas!* (Mecca is finished!)" Their hilarity would not abate.

I was reminded of my father's story about the siege of Mecca in 1979 and the subsequent rise of al-Qaeda. The insurgents had attempted to take over the Grand Mosque and its control from the Saudi government. As odd as it was for a Muslim group to attack Mecca, there was plenty of precedent for it. The Houthis were no different than the many other preceding Muslim groups of outliers.

Azziz had not participated in the drugs. He said, "You see what's happening? Do you know what's in the middle of the room? The Persians have been foolish."

The impossible finally came to me. The large metal case contained the bomb. Azziz's comportment toward me continued to change. Now that I knew about the weapon and their intended use of it, I could not be allowed to communicate outside Yemen. How could they afford to let me leave at all?

CHAPTER 11

WILL THEY BOMB MECCA?

The connections began to make sense. It was the Persians, the Houthis, and ISIL pitted against Saudi Arabia. They were going to bomb Mecca. Where was Esau in all this? Then it hit me. Esau was involved because they were all going to blame the Christians. Of course. Now I knew why he was the intermediary. Esau had made the connections among the groups, and he was set on achieving his agenda—the destruction of all religion in the Middle East. He no longer needed to be physically present. He would get at Christians, and also the various Muslim groups at the same time, through these strange intermediaries.

The drug orgy in the hotel basement continued for several hours while I sat under Azziz's observation. At 2 in the morning, he accompanied me to my room, unplugged the phone from the wall, and took it with him. He knew the landline was more dependable than the spotty cell reception. Tahara would be expecting a call, but there was no means to make it.

I turned on the TV and listened for a while to the pointless news, while trying to figure out a way of getting word about the bomb to the outside world. By 4 a.m., the hotel was quiet. The guard sitting outside my door, head bowed, and slumped was bellowing with snores, and I sneaked down to the lobby. A group of BBC and Reuters reporters were gathered at their computers with cigarettes and several bottles of Scotch of their own importation. The late hour guaranteed the forbidden alcohol use would go undetected—at least by anyone who mattered. There next to one of the men was a small, brown satellite phone in a charging case. I startled the man from his stupor. "May I use your phone?"

He was too drunk to ask why. "Yeah, sure man. Just don't call my wife."

I phoned Tahara first, "Why are you calling so late? Your father is very sick. I think it's best you come home."

"There's no way I can come now. I have to tell you what's happening here. You have to listen and write down what I tell you. I'm in the Taj Aswan Hotel in Hodeidah. The Houthis have a nuclear weapon in the basement. They plan to ignite the bomb in Mecca and blame the Christians in the Gulf. You've got to tell your contacts at Al Jazeera so they can get the message to the Americans. I don't know how much time we have. The Houthis are crazy. There's no one really in control. I'm sure they'll try to use the bomb."

Tahara responded, "Of course, I know just who to call. Yusef, you've got to get out of there."

"Now that I know about the bomb, they won't let me leave. I

love you. Tell my father I love him. I have to go now."

Then I phoned Khadim in Tehran. He picked up the call out of sleep. "Why are you calling me? Do you know the time?"

"Khadim, all your tricks have come to trouble. First, I have to tell you the Houthis are sending your money to ISIL."

"You can't be serious! We'll stop the funds right away. I told the Supreme Leader we couldn't trust them."

"But there's more. The bomb you sent them? They're going to use it to bomb Mecca. They're really going to do it. I've sent a message to the Americans. I hope they'll come for it soon."

"You've told the Americans. I can't believe it. That spells disaster. The Americans are coming to get a piece of trash. Did you think we were foolish enough to really give those madmen the bomb? We sent them a version of the W87, but the device contains no plutonium or uranium. There would be an initial chemical explosion but no nuclear detonation. We had to retain control. We only planned to give them the necessary components if there were specific circumstances that arose." And what were those *specific circumstances*? He did not say.

The conversation was over, and we both hung up. The damage was done. The BBC reporter was asleep or unconscious. I put the satellite phone back in the case and retreated to my room. I would have called Tahara to give her news of Khadim's information, but I knew the sooner the Americans got there, the more likely I would survive and be rescued.

At 7 a.m., Azziz pounded on my door. "Breakfast now." He was no longer polite; and it was clear I was officially a prisoner, though still without chains. He said, "We must remain in Hodeidah. We think you're safe here, safe from communicating with friends. We have to decide what to do with you."

"Azziz, I have to go back to Kuwait. My father is very sick."

"I'm very sorry, but you are now on vacation here by the Red Sea. We can go for a swim in the cool sea today if you like."

For several hours we walked along the beach. Hodeidah was still a fishing village, even though the catch from the Red Sea was greatly diminished. The Egyptians had tried to minimize commercial fishing in order to preserve the reefs and colorful fish for their tourists, but the Yemenis, having few tourists, declined to participate. Red coral grouper, triggerfish, yellow butterflyfish, and freckled hawkfish were displayed on wooden tables. The Egyptian tourists further north at Sharm Al Sheikh would miss them.

When we reached a stretch of sand away from the fishermen, we stripped down to trousers and went for a swim. We had no snorkeling equipment, but the water was clear and there were a few fish near the shore for our entertainment. Under other circumstances, I would have enjoyed Azziz's company. We walked back the way we had come and asked the fish sellers to grill some of their catch for us. When we got to the hotel, Azziz told me I was to stay in my room the remainder of the evening. The young, sleepy Houthi was again assigned a position outside my door.

I didn't think it would take long. I watched TV to keep me

awake while waiting for the Americans. Surely the Navy Seals would rescue me.

But I heard nothing until 6 a.m. the next morning when Azizz pounded on my door. He was angry and aggressive. His first words were, "Come with me. I want you to see what your friends have done." He and another Houthi whom I had not met before took me by the arm, and we descended the steps into the basement room. There on the floor in a field of blood were six young Houthis. Their throats had been cut from the front completely through to their spines. I could see the exposed white bone of the vertebrae. The bomb container was gone. "See what you've done! Three of these men had families. Who will care for their women and children?" The others quickly began the process of gathering and washing the bodies for their burial within the prescribed twenty-four-hour period.

I was taken back to my room where coffee and fresh bread awaited. Azziz's last words were, "We have to decide what to do with you." I never saw him again.

My hope of rescue by the Americans evaporated. My own importance did not match up with the bomb, and the special forces had rescued the bomb and left me behind.

The BBC reporters, working in the alcove of the lobby were up early, sober, and clicking away on their computers. They said they were doing a background piece on the Houthi movement. About 10 a.m., one of the reporters emitted a cry of dismay as he spoke to his editor. I heard, "What do you mean we missed the story right under us? There's nothing going on here." Then to his colleagues, he said, "They're sending us the Al Jazeera report right now. I can't believe I'm reading this." The reporters gathered about the screen. When I asked in English to see the screen, they allowed me to join them.

The report was titled, "Kuwaiti Parliament Member Saves Mecca from Nuclear Bomb" and read, "Last night the city of Mecca was saved from a nuclear explosion. A member of the Kuwait Parliament, Yusef Al-Tamimi, who was visiting Yemen as his country's envoy, discovered the Houthi plot to explode a nuclear device in the holy city of Mecca. Al Jazeera has learned from unnamed sources that the bomb was provided to the Yemenis by Iran. The Persians were planning to blame Christian extremists. Al-Tamimi was able to get the information to the necessary recipients, and the attack to get possession of the bomb proceeded quickly. The U.S.S. Iwo Jima, an amphibious assault ship, was moved out of the Gulf of Aden and into the Red Sea just off the city of Hodeidah. A twenty man Special Forces Unit landed on the beach in the early hours, proceeded to the Taj Aswan Hotel where they encountered only minimal resistance, and captured the nuclear device. The bomb was taken back to the Iwo Jima where it was disarmed.

"Al Jazeera has attempted to reach Mr. Al-Tamimi, the hero of Mecca, but he has not responded."

The BBC reporters turned to me, "Are you Al-Tamimi?" Fearing my identification would make my situation worse, I didn't reply, turned, and went for the stairs. I was too paralyzed to interact with them. Should I involve the reporters? They'd probably be killed if they intervened. I had to get home; and now it was going to be even more difficult. I tried to summon the courage to make a break for it. But where and how would I go?

The world loves a dramatic story, even if it isn't true. By this time the Americans certainly knew, along with the Iranians, that there was no functional nuclear device, but the United States wanted it known they had helped save Mecca, and the Iranians didn't want their allies to know they had distributed a fake bomb. I was a hero without a good deed.

I sunk further into despair, and the trap I was in fed my outward anguish in every way. The Houthis apparently couldn't afford to let me go. But my inner distress was worse. When it came right down to it, I wasn't certain the Lord was in charge. "When shall I come and appear before God? My tears have been my food day and night, while they say to me all the day long, 'Where is your God?'" (Psalm 42:2b-3). I was the one asking, "Where is God?"

I missed Azziz. He was the one constant I had experienced in my short time in Yemen. I speculated he was being punished for allowing the capture of the bomb. Two muscular, mostly unspeaking young men now replaced him. Their immediate job was only to see that I was fed and that I did not venture off on my own. The next morning, I asked, "May we return to Sana'a now?" Although I knew they understood, they did not respond.

At 7 a.m. on the morning of the third day of my detention by the Houthis, I was awakened by the noisy departure of a number of vehicles from the hotel. Pulling the tattered curtain and looking out the window, I saw the Houthis driving off in convoy. My first sentiment was that of reprieve and liberation, but a series of forceful knocks on the door replaced that emotion. There were repetitions of the phrase *"Allahu akbar!"* (God is the greatest!) When I opened the door, three men dressed in black were laughing. The oldest said, "May God be praised. You are now the prisoner of ISIL. For what you have done, you will pay with captivity and your head, but first you will have breakfast."

The recollection of my dream came back. I had dreamed of some sort of capture and prolonged confinement, and now it was upon me. What would the knife feel like on my neck? After my head was severed from my body, would I have a brief moment of remaining awareness?

My breakfast was monitored in the hotel basement by a band of black-dressed young men who ate voraciously for perhaps thirty minutes. Then the camera and newspaper were brought out. The men covered their faces with black cloths up to their eyes, lined up on either side of me, and handed me the newspaper of the day to hold for the photograph. The newspaper showed the date, and the dress of the men demonstrated I was now held by ISIL. Following the photograph, I was told to get my bag as we prepared to leave. When we went outside there were ten vehicles, three Toyota Tacomas with .50 caliber Browning machine guns mounted in the back, three Humvees, and four assorted older vehicles of uncertain make. I was put in one of the Humvees, blindfolded, and we were off. The men were singing and excited. Before my eyes were covered, I saw several taking the Captagon pills.

As we rode off, I felt a man hold each of my arms; my right sleeve was rolled up, and a piece of rubber tubing was tied and tightened above the elbow in order to distend my blood vessels. Then, a needle entered my vein. I soon experienced nausea and thought I was going to vomit. Then I felt nothing, heard nothing, saw nothing. I don't know how long I was unconscious.

When I began to regain my senses, it was cool and I could sense the vehicle was traveling rapidly on a winding road. We stopped a short while after I roused, and they removed my blindfold and allowed me to urinate. I looked out into the night strewn with thousands of stars. From the clarity of stars, I concluded we were far from the bright lights from any large city. I could see a small collection of lights in the valley far below. We must have been traveling in the mountains. I was taken into a three-story building that looked as if tourists had frequented it in years past. There were hand-sewn carpets nailed onto the walls with an old saddle in the far corner, the decorations of a former tourist era. The men with me kept their faces covered and called out for the owner, who soon appeared out of the rear of the building. "As-*Salaam-Alai-kum!*" (Peace be unto you!) was offered.

And the expected response echoed back "*Wa-Alaikum-Salaam!*" (And unto you peace!) Rice and beans were brought out and I ate along with my captors. Then, we climbed the stone staircase with steps of unequal height, which I now recognized as typical of its ancient construction. I was given a small room with a tiny window, too small to squeeze out of, and the door clanged tight, locked from the outside. The night grew cold, and I struggled to stay warm on the floor without a blanket. The masked men offered no information about the coming day.

We rose early the next morning and consumed fresh bread with tea. Then my blindfold was replaced, and we were off again, traveling curvy roads. By midday, they removed my blindfold. There was no chance I could retrace any of the route or identify our location by the visible surroundings. We were ascending a poorly maintained two-lane road. We occasionally passed other vehicles, usually small, antique pickup trucks, but also large trucks hauling heavy supplies. The driver had no hesitation passing on curves without knowledge of oncoming vehicles. When I challenged his method, he informed me that, if there was enough room for two vehicles, there was enough room for three. *But what if the oncoming vehicles had the same mindset? Was there enough room for four?*

By this time the rest of the convoy had long disappeared, and we drove on alone. Two of my three unnamed, masked guards discussed my future as if I were not present.

"He must wonder where we're taking him. Does it matter if we tell him?"

"What could it matter? He'll never return from his visit." He laughed.

"Will they tell us to keep him here?"

"Perhaps. But the decision must be made whether he is to live or die. *'In shā' Allāh* (as God wills). We must follow orders. He will remain in this village for a time."

Shortly after that, we pulled off the paved road and onto a barely perceptible rocky path leading up into the peaks. The former road up the mountain had been bombed out, and the squeaky little truck struggled over rocks too large for its wheels. I hoped the truck would not make the climb. Of course, my hope had no realistic objective. The path leveled out after about an hour, and we entered a group of old stone buildings built around the top of the mountain.

We wound our way through the narrows streets and then paths until we arrived at a two story, gray building of irregular, and apparently unplanned, construction. The structure was on the downhill slope, making it necessary that the stones of its edifice had been laid accordingly. The single entry was a wooden arch less than five feet high. We entered the inner darkness that smelled of a wood fire. As my eyes became accustomed to the low light, I saw two women over a cooking pot and three small children. The women had hastily covered themselves as we entered, looked down, and did not speak. The children had large heads and small bodies with swollen abdomens. There had been no attempts at cleanliness, and their acrid body smell staggered me.

I was taken up the stone stairs and placed in a room with a mat covering a pile a straw. A bowl lay in one corner and a bucket in another. The taller man spat on the floor where I would sleep and said, "This is your new home." Then they left me there. The room had no door that could be closed so I was not caged in any way. I was not relieved by the lack of a door. I had no idea how to get out of this village without someone seeing me; and even if I could, where would I go?

Even so, as my captors drove down the mountain, I immediately began to consider escape. However, escape implied I knew what direction to go once I left the village. We had traveled hours by truck to get here, and I had no idea where I was.

I went back down the stairs to the smoky kitchen, where the women looked down at their steaming pots, avoiding my eye contact. The oldest boy took my hand, led me into an area between the buildings, and brought out a ball made of twine that had been wound tightly into a sphere. He demonstrated that we were to engage in a soccer game as other boys joined. We exchanged conversation, and I discovered their Arabic dialect differed significantly from my own.

After about an hour of soccer, I saw the first men of the village. Two approached and we sat in the afternoon sun as a little girl brought tea. One identified himself as Seyed, and the second declined to state his name. Seyed proceeded to state the conditions of my presence there. "You are here as our guest. You will be treated as such, unless you attempt to leave. If you attempt, we will have to chain you. Even if you escape our village, you don't know where to go, so you might as well enjoy your life here among us."

"But I have family in Kuwait that I must see. They need me."

"We are your family now. The Zaidi are a happy people."

I interjected, "ISIL brought me here. How is it you have traffic with them?"

Seyed responded, "We use them. They use us. It's only temporary. Soon, *In shā᾽ Allāh,* we will be free." How would they ever be free?

I found his answers unsatisfactory. The Zaidis, of course, were Shia, albeit Fivers rather than the more common Twelvers, and ISIL was of the strictest Wahhabi tradition. Why had ISIL left me in the hands of Zaidis?

The tea grew cold and still we sat watching the sun recede. Of course, the qat came out and Seyed and his companion proceeded first to the qat-induced levity, and then as the light of the sun disappeared completely, they sank into a half stupor. With all this poverty, still there was the qat. I saw a cell phone protruding from Seyed's pocket. I reached for it, but he awoke with a shiver and grabbed my hand. "You aren't permitted to call anyone. Besides, there's no service here on our mountain." *Then why was he carrying the phone?* I remained in the dark.

For a week the routine became established: the unspeaking women who remained covered in my presence, the filthy little children who engaged me, Seyed and his nameless friends with their tea and qat, and looking out over the endless peaks.

Piecing together the appearance of the area and the length of our drive to the region, I concluded we must be in the Haraz Mountains, which rest in the northwest corner of Yemen about 100 kilometers from Sana'a. That conclusion didn't help. There was no reasonable means of escape. And further, I had no way of knowing the nature or the intensity of the international search for me, the hero of Mecca. Was there any search at all?

At the end of the first week, one of the women, Zaynab, spoke her first words to me. She had removed the covering from her face. "I'm sorry for the food we give you. We have no more or anything better ourselves. I don't get as much as you. I'm Seyed's fourth wife."

She saw me looking at the scar that enveloped the entire left side of her face. "I fell into the fire when I was a child. I have the falling sickness." By this I understood she was epileptic. "They say I have a bad spirit in me, but I know a have a spirit of hope." What a statement from this young woman bereft of all material possessions.

Seyed entered the room, and Zaynab withdrew. Seyed said, "She is useless as a wife, but she's a good worker."

The next two days I spent walking about the village and looking off into the valley. There was only one usable, main path down the mountain. From that path other smaller ones branched out into the fields for gathering firewood and to the terraced areas where the qat and coffee were cultivated. Each morning the women took these trails to their required work. The men took the donkeys for plowing and the older children herded the sheep and goats.

If I could escape, I would need to navigate the paths less traveled; and then upon reaching the paved road, avoid the vehicles I might encounter. And what about water? I couldn't carry enough with me. Every exit I considered depended upon my making connection with other people. Would they choose to help me or turn me in? Should I just set out walking and hope for the best? The task seemed impossible, and the hope ridiculous. "My God, my God, why have you forsaken me? Why are you so far from saving me, from the words of my groaning? O my God, I cry by day, but you do not answer, and by night, but I find no rest" (Psalm 22:1-2). The subsequent verses of the same psalm plagued me: "Yet you are holy, enthroned on the praises of Israel. In you our father trusted; they trusted, and you delivered them" (Psalm 22:3-4). I wondered if the latter verses applied to me, an Arab.

When we were alone, Zaynab said to me, "You're planning to escape, aren't you? They'll kill you. And if you escape, ISIL will kill us all. I heard them tell that to Seyed. Seyed is a fool, and ISIL is the Devil himself. We've sold ourselves to them by agreeing to hold you. We heard you're one of the People of the Book. You need to know there are strange things happening here in Al Bijar" That was the first time I had heard the name of the village.

"What things, the strange things?"

"I've had a dream, many times the same dream. God comes for me. He takes me away from this awful place, where there is only soot from the cooking, dust from the fields, and cruelty from the man who owns me. When God takes me away, the scar on my face is gone." For a moment she was transformed. It was the first time I saw her stand erect. "A man came to our village. He spoke only to the women while the men were gone. He told us of Isa. He told me it was Isa who came for me. We can't read, so there was no point in his leaving us the books in his knapsack, but he taught us a saying, a powerful one: "For God so loved the world, that he gave his only Son, that whoever believes in him should not perish but have eternal life" (John 3:16). He told me God sent His Son Isa for me."

I was silent. As always, the gospel had outpaced me. Even here on a high mountain in the kingdom of the Devil, God had penetrated.

"The man told us (the few women he spoke to) that we are now the People of the Return, the People of the Return of Isa. We told others about what happened to us, and some have told their husbands. Several were beaten because of Isa."

I couldn't understand how she could believe on the basis of so little information. She knew she was Zaidi, but beyond the name of her tribe she knew little. She didn't know the Zaidi were a branch of the Shia. She didn't know how the Shia differed from the rest of Islam, but somehow the phrase, People of the Return, had penetrated this mountain, and its effect had been profound on this woman.

I continued in a quandary about whether I ought to attempt an escape. I didn't know the way to safety, if there was any. And I didn't want to be responsible for the deaths of these poor people, these poverty-laden people who had bound themselves to ISIL.

The puzzle was solved for me when the three ISIL men returned the next morning in their white Tacoma. We retraced the rocky trail from the village and back to the main road. The three men no longer bothered to cover their faces. With the morning sun off to my left, it was now clear we were driving south.

They did not blindfold me. I took this as a sign that my witness no longer mattered, and that they intended to kill me. I was beyond being frightened. Fear had transformed to another emotion I couldn't identify. Courage? No, not that, not me. We continued south, and I thought we were headed back to Aden, but we turned west at Al-Bayda, and soon we were traveling along the coast of the Gulf of Aden. We arrived at the small port city of Mukalla. In contrast to Hodeidah with its dirt, dust, and scattered plastic bags, Mukalla was a gleaming city of many white buildings placed immediately next to the blue sea and backed by rocky, gray cliffs.

I finally asked my captors, "Why did you take me away from the Zaidis?"

"Al-Baghdadi said you're worth more in our possession. The Saudis and Kuwaitis will pay for you. What does it matter to you? We'll likely kill you anyway, you're a *keffer* (unbeliever)."

From that time my detention continued for many days and alternately consisted of an unpredictable variation of being chained in a dark room to roaming about the little seaport with my captors. For my room, they chose a white stone building on the outskirts of Mukalla near the northern part of the city where the road began to ascend into the rocky hills. The small window of my room was covered from the outside by shutters, allowing only minimal light. The door was locked, and my wrists and ankles were chained. The chains were for my discomfort only, as I could not have escaped through the locked door anyway. On two occasions bright lights were brought into the room and I was photographed in chains with the masked captor holding a newspaper of the day for dating. In the second session, one of the men held a large knife over my neck as if to demonstrate my impending execution. This mode of terrorism exhibition had been used repetitively by ISIL to the point that its impact had become routine among the news media. While the knife rested on my carotid artery, another psalm came to me. "For behold, the wicked bend the bow; they have fitted their arrow to the string to shoot in the dark at the upright in heart; if the foundations are destroyed, what can the righteous do?" (Psalm 11:2-3). Only psalms of sadness and regret emerged from my memory. I was inconsolable.

On another day my three jailers took me along almost as a colleague as we meandered about the city on the sea. Fishing was good, and the shoreline markets boasted a large assortment of fish, most not known to me. They asked one of the vendors to carve off a slab from a large yellowfin tuna. There on the beach, the vendor grilled the fresh fish, and we gorged ourselves on the half raw tuna along with bread, beans, and rice.

The juxtaposition of chain days, which were the most common, with beach days led to increased disorientation, which apparently was their design. This odd routine continued for nearly six weeks. All told, I calculated the total length of my custody at over two months so far.

On June 10, 2024, they allowed me to call Tahara. They were right by my side, making it impossible for me to reveal my location. "Tahara, they're allowing me one call. I miss you."

She began to cry immediately. "Yusef, your father has died. We buried him in the same graveyard as your mother." More Muslim territory had thus been claimed for Jesus. And I had had nothing to do with it, as usual.

They cut off my call after three minutes. Tahara and I had not finished speaking. She had not sounded as brave as I imagined, but she was able to finish without more tears.

My attendant entered my darkened room earlier than usual the next morning. "You should be very proud. Al-Baghdadi says you're worth 100 million euros. When they pay, you might be released. *'In shā' Allāh.*'"

The man in charge in the hallway countered that with, "You won't be released. The end is soon, but for the time we need you." They had collaborated in their confusing prediction.

All the psalms I had recently recalled were the "songs of lament" that questioned the future action of God. Now, as my anger seeped out over my circumstance, the memories of my mother forced my mind to the psalms, calling down the vengeance of Lord instead: "O my God, in you I trust; let me not be put to shame; let not my enemies exult over me" (Psalm 25:2b). Surely God saw my plight and would act on my behalf. *Was my faith increasing?*

In two days, my team of captors told me the news, "The Saudi and Kuwaiti governments have agreed to pay the demand. You must be important to them. We know you're an expert in transfer-

151

ring funds from our spies' reports. We'll need your assistance in getting the funds to the proper accounts." So they were computer illiterate. "Our man will arrive tomorrow to make sure you follow instructions properly."

The following morning my supposed transfer monitor arrived. It was Kulabali. He gave no indication we knew each other, and of course, I did not either. A computer was produced, and after an extended wait, a slowly functioning landline was established. The transfer of fifty million euros from each of the Saudi and Kuwait governments appeared, and we were given the routing and account numbers for the ISIL account. As I put in the numbers, Kulabali distracted the ISIL captors by spilling his hot coffee in their laps. Then, with only two quick keystrokes he erased the ISIL numbers, placed another set into the system, and I entered the transaction.

As Kulabali prepared to leave, he whispered that a rescue team would arrive at 2 in the morning, and I should be ready. I pulled him back into my room. With courage I did not possess, I said, "I'm not leaving."

"What do you mean?"

"I'm not leaving. Something good must come from all this. I'm going back to Al Bajar to get Zaynab and her friends."

"That's madness. There's no way to do this. We have no way to get there, and we have no papers to pass the checkpoints. They'll kill you, maybe me, too."

"You'll have to make this happen, or I'm not leaving. You have to do this. You must have the connections. You've gotten this far."

He surprised me again. He said, "OK." *Was there a little laugh?*

I'd given up myself as lost. Even though I wanted to rescue Zaynab, I saw no realistic way to accomplish this. *What was I thinking?* But Kulabali was still there for me. "Alright, be watchful tonight." As he left the Mukalla hotel on his motorcycle, he said to me quietly, "Thanks to us, the People of the Return are richer today. You must take care. They'll know soon."

That afternoon the ISIL men burst into my room. "You've cheated our leader. The money is gone. Where did it go? You must tell us." They beat me worse than anything I had experienced in the Iranian prisons. Would I father more children? I had no concern about the bruises on my face. "We have been instructed to execute you tomorrow. Tonight will be your last night on earth. As a kindness, we won't chain you."

I was emboldened by the moment. "What if I did tell you where the money went? It doesn't matter. The money is gone."

I waited. At 1 a.m., an old white pickup, headlights off, pulled up quietly in front of the hotel. There were four adult sheep tethered in the bed of the truck and a ram in the jump seat. Kulabali, dressed as a Yemeni, and a dirty one at that, got out and entered the building. After a brief scuffle in the hall, he came into my room and handed me the necessary escape outfit. My guard was dead with his throat cut completely through, just like the young Houthis in the basement who had guarded the bomb.

The streets of Mukalla were deserted and dark. Kulabali started the truck and the two of us, plus the five sheep, were off into the night. I soon got used to the smelly breath of the ram crowded into the back seat. I took comfort in the animal. He was part of our disguise—two Yemenis taking their animals to market. I looked at Kulabali. He didn't look back. All I could see was his set jaw and worried expression.

We proceeded west along the road I had used in entering the city. We approached the first checkpoint, this one manned by Houthi tribesmen. We were now both dressed as poor Yemenis. Kulabali gave me a wad of qat to put in my cheek, and he produced our papers. I was Nasser Al-Murra, and he was Abdullah Al-Qadi. How strange that he had chosen for me a Kuwaiti tribal name.

So it went for two days. We had to stop periodically to feed and water the sheep. We entered the Haraz mountains and then finally the outskirts of Al-Bajar at night. Kulabali parked the truck, let the sheep loose, and we entered the outskirts of the town. He brought out a satellite phone I had not seen, and got online. There was a minute of chatter, and we waited. An hour later, we heard the rotation of a helicopter rotor in the distance, and then two rocket-propelled grenades exploded harmlessly outside the city; the explosion was as bright as fire in the dark night. Men in confusion began to emerge from the stone houses.

Amidst the confusion, I saw Zaynab. I ran to her and told her our mission. She didn't hesitate. She pulled two women out of the crowd and we bent down to the ground behind two large boulders. The mission I thought had no chance of success was succeeding.

The smelly smoke from the explosions, the resulting haze, and the tumult among the people all contributed to the frightening disorder. The men of the village ran for their weapons, ancient single-shot rifles, but they didn't know where to shoot.

The helicopter fired another grenade into an area without people, and then a second helicopter appeared and landed near us. Kulabali was on the radio constantly.

We boarded the craft and took off amid the rising dust and disorder. Zaynab and her two friends cowered in the back of the copter, a flying creature they had never been inside before. After thirty minutes we arrived at the U.S.S Firebolt, where a female Navy physician examined me. I phoned Tahara and told her I was safe.

"I can't believe it. The Lord preserved you."

"How is the pregnancy?" She informed me she was a little sick at times, but doing well.

Over the next two days, the ship made its way out of the Red Sea, through the Gulf of Aden, and into the Strait of Hormuz to the American military base in Qatar. The three women from the village stayed to themselves like frightened sheep. Who could blame them? They had just been vaulted into another century. We were flown to Kuwait, where there was an unimaginable hero's welcome for me—even a large Kuwaiti army detachment in their dress greens. The emir and his entourage met me briefly at the airport, and then he was off. He had reaped the advantage of sending a hero on a mission and that was enough.

Zaynab and her two friends were taken to the home of a wealthy church member. We knew they were in for culture shock of the first order. Their faces were like stone.

The *Kuwait Times* headline was "Kuwaiti Christian Saves Mecca." Of course Mecca was never in danger from the fake bomb, but none of the participants could reveal this without appearing foolish.

I saw changes accelerating at a rapid rate.

CHAPTER 12

THE GULF STATES SHAKE

Applause and a standing ovation met me on my return to the floor of the Kuwaiti Parliament. Their sustained clapping generated air currents in the tightly packed hall, and the smell of mixed colognes wafted over the scene. A sea of dark beards and white dishdashas marked the event in my memory. Many of my colleagues were smiling, but many were not, and I suspected the smiles of some were for appearances rather than genuine congratulations.

But the first day was mine, and the news media consumed the photos and stories of my heroic deeds. I was a hero of circumstance due to my capture by ISIL. The ninety-five-degree temperature didn't discourage the train of media cars following me to Ahmadi. The humidity was high for spring, and my shirt was drenched when I reached home.

The end of the day found our home surrounded by reporters from news networks including BBC, Fox, CNN and Al-Jazeera. Each network displayed its own logo, and the colors among them failed to match. The irony of a Christian saving Mecca was too juicy to be ignored.

I accepted questions from all. The Fox news reporter asked, "How did your Christian faith support you when you were held by ISIL?"

To many present the question seemed foolish, but not to me. I fumbled the answer like a politician. Why did they ask that? Surely, I had grown in the Lord somewhat, and I had survived the captivity. My response lacked specifics: "Yes, of course my faith supported me." I turned to the next reporter in line without giving him a chance for a follow-up. I did not know what else to say. How does one measure his own faith?

Out of the large group of reporters, we invited the Al Jazeera representative into our home. Tahara knew the young man, Albert Quinton, who was the chief reporter for Gulf political affairs. He went right to the crux of the matter. How would these recent events affect the governments of the Gulf? I had been away for some time. Were things worse?

"Mr. Al-Tamimi, I know you must be exhausted from the occurrences of the last few months, but we would like to know the political significance of what has happened." I wanted to avoid that discussion too. I had had enough. "Much of the conflict is between Sunni and Shia. What do you make of ISIL's entrance into the scene? Who would have suffered most from the ISIL plan to bomb Mecca? It failed, but it could have succeeded."

Tahara and I looked at each other. We knew there were risks in any answer. I asked for the Lord's help, something I had not done earlier with such clarity. "Incline your ear to me; rescue me speedily! Be a rock of refuge for me, a strong fortress to save me!" (Psalm 31:2).

I said too much. "The first question is why did ISIL want to destroy Mecca. From an Islamic standpoint, it makes no sense, which means their plan must not have had anything to do with Islam. The reason must be political. ISIL has no confidence in the Sunni leadership of Saudi Arabia, and certainly not in the leadership of the other Gulf States. They want that role for themselves. More than that I do not know, and those are only guesses."

Tahara once again touched my hand, this time in an effort to restrain me. Still, I went on. "If the Saudis can't protect Mecca and the Kaaba, they can't be the perpetual guardians of the seat of Mohammed either." *Now I'd done it.* "ISIL is therefore the enemy of the old guard Sunni establishment because the old guard Sunnis in Mecca have failed. Saudi Arabia's young leader, Mohammed bin Salman, has shown his colors. He wants it all. Where does this leave the rest of the Gulf rulers? The other Gulf States are all painted with the same brush." For the moment, my courage rose. The faith manifest here was not from me. "If the current Sunni leadership can't protect the heart of Islam and the rest of the Gulf from ISIL, who remains? Who benefits? It must be the rest, the Shia and the Christians in the Gulf. At least that's how it looks to me."

Quinton continued, "What's left of Sunni Islam in the Gulf?"

Again my answer was probably too pointed. "The Sunni governments in the Gulf aren't up to fending off ISIL. The social com-

159

ponent of Sunni Islam only remains as a shell." Tahara showed no expression but her lips were pale.

"What about Shia Islam?"

"Shia Islam remains untouched by these trials. They've not forsaken their roots. ISIL attempted to cheat the Zaidi Shia and the Houthis. They used them, or tried to use them for their own devices. The Shias are the minority in the Gulf, but they've stayed true to their basic beliefs. They're poor for two reasons: The first reason is that they don't seek worldly wealth." This was an exaggeration. The Shia wanted money and things just like the rest of us. "The second reason is that their position in Muslim society is controlled for the benefit of the Sunnis." This was completely true.

The reporter followed up with his last question. "You sound very pessimistic about the future of the Sunni leadership in the Gulf. What does this all mean for the political situation in the Gulf?"

"*'In shā' Allāh.*" He must have known I had to avoid that question.

The reporter departed with a handshake, a headshake, and a slight bow. By this time the other reporters were gone, and the evening sunset diffused in an orange-red sky. A sandstorm was approaching.

Tahara waited until the reporter had left. To this point she had kept her concerns restrained. "How can you say these things so bluntly, and to a reporter who is obligated to turn in what you say on the record? You have a responsibility to protect our family now. It's not just you anymore."

I was confused. "I thought you wanted me to take the lead and fight for what we think is right."

Holding her abdomen with both hands, Tahara sank down in the big chair, the one my father had loved. "I don't know what I want," she sighed.

The Kuwait TV news did not report my remarks, but the local Gulf Al Jazeera network gave an accurate account of my statements, and then the Kuwait newspapers picked up the Al Jazeera text. An article on page three of the *Kuwait Times* read, "Nothing Remains of Gulf Sunni Leadership but the Social Shell Says Al-Tamimi."

Gossip rumbled through the community that Esau was responsible for the ISIL connection, but my half-brother Esau was never physically present at any of the events described by the media. Binyamin took advantage and set the rumor corridor of the Internet afire with news of the Esau connection. Blogs, signed by unknown bloggers, appeared, describing how Esau had engineered the connection between Iran and ISIL. Twitter accounts of similar origin appeared and flashed around among Kuwaitis on social media. Esau phoned me from the United States and threatened reprisals, but I feigned ignorance as to how the social media threads had appeared.

###

My father's church had survived his death and thrived. Thawab, my half-brother, took over as pastor. My published comments had mixed effects on the church. Those who were faithful but fearful stopped attending for a time, but others who had comprised small house churches came out in large numbers and began attending under Thawab's leadership. Among the new attendees were Zaynab and her two companions who had fled the oppression of Al-Bajar. Still bewildered by the transformations around them, the three women had been slowly immersed into the Christian community. They emulated the other church members by bowing their heads and later lifting their hands.

Threats did not restrain the gospel. The number of cars parked around the church exceeded the capacity of the neighborhood, and the families whose residences were around there came out of their homes to complain to the church attendees. The encounters were cordial at first.

Tahara was one of the fearful. In retrospect I believe this reaction was due to her pregnancy, but she declined to attend the church until the baby was delivered. I tried to comfort her in her rare time of weakness, but failed.

Meanwhile threats of varying degrees continued against my family. The next week a small packaged bomb was thrown over the wall and into our garden near the altar my father had built. Brown smoke rolled around the garden, and it smelled like firecrackers. There was no shrapnel and little damage, but I was angry. One colleague in parliament asked, "Did you plant the bomb to draw further attention to yourself?" This accusation struck me as so peculiar that I didn't even get made mad about it. He was a fool, and he was lucky I didn't hit him, an impulse very uncharacteristic of a rich, Kuwaiti Arab.

Three masked men dressed in black attacked Thawab after church the next week. They waited in the church until the crowd had left, and Thawab remained to lock the building. Thawab was a sturdy combatant with military training, but they overpowered him with clubs. He was in the Ahmadi hospital for two days. He left the hospital with bandages around both forearms, the result of his holding up his arms for defense. The bandages looked impressive in a photograph on page three of the newspaper.

Binyamin was fired from his computer programing position at the Bank of Kuwait and the Middle East. His boss gave no reason, just "belt tightening." He was, of course, saddened by his removal, but he was resourceful and confident in the progress of the gospel. We suspected Esau was behind his dismissal. Binyamin had been dogging Esau electronically for months, and we had expected reprisal.

Tahara was run off the road by a black Jeep. Her sturdy Mercedes preserved her and the baby, but her fear grew, and my anger increased exponentially. I wanted God to intervene. "God shall arise…As smoke is driven away, so you shall drive them away; as wax melts before the fire, so the wicked shall perish before God!" (Psalm 68:1-2). I waited for God to act, but not patiently.

Quinton from Al Jazeera returned to our Ahmadi home for a follow-up interview. He was apologetic about our recent events.

"I'm sorry to trouble you and your family, but you've become the focus of many of the ongoing conflicts. How are you doing?" We answered with barely mustered pleasantries. "Who do you think is responsible for the recent attacks on your family?"

"We don't know for certain, most likely random Sunnis who want retribution. If it was ISIL, we wouldn't have survived." We didn't mention Esau.

"Who do think will come out on top in the Gulf."

My answer would incur condemnation from many quarters. "The real power in the Gulf is Iran." Quinton did not look up, avoiding my gaze. "Their vast diversity will come out eventually. Their so-called Supreme Leader can't restrain it. They won't use the bomb. Just possessing the bomb is sufficient. They have everything they need to be a great country." The Arabs of the Gulf were already afraid of the Persians.

The other news media picked up my quote. There was nothing I could say that could make things worse. In the eyes of many, I had betrayed the Gulf leadership, and even the Arab race itself. Had I become a Persian?

I could no longer speak in a meaningful way on any subject in parliament. Any position I took evoked the opposite response in my colleagues. I remained quiet the rest of my term. I voted on the various bills that came up, and my colleagues could only hope my vote was the opposite of their own. The usual course for a member of parliament was to run again for the next term. There was no point for me to do this, and in 2025 my term would be concluded.

Tahara and I were both afraid to use the public hospitals. Ephraim was born at the British Medical Centre on the Ahmadi Expressway. Genesis 41:52 said this of Joseph's choice of the name Ephraim, "It is because God has made me fruitful in the land of my suffering." I had suffered much less than many others, and suffering would accelerate for some, but I considered my very preservation a sign of the Lord's faithfulness.

###

The emir caught wind of a plan to rewrite the constitution, and the next parliamentary election was suspended along with the parliament itself. Such attempts at reform had occurred in the past, but this time the emir recognized that the threat was genuine. His advisors correctly informed him the will of the people changed. Citizens were afraid the leadership could no longer protect them from invading influences, mainly ISIL, but also Iran. He knew if the country proceeded in its current direction, more trouble would be instigated for the Sunni leadership. He called me to the palace. "Yusef, are you behind this new constitution idea." I wasn't, and I told him that. I thought he believed me. For reasons unknown to me, the emir still trusted me.

The world news agencies picked up the story as if the suspension of parliament had never before happened in Kuwait. In fact, most Kuwaitis had lost count of such occasions. The news photographed the emir and his entourage departing for London on his personal jet. Their group was not small. Yet his departure was nothing out of the ordinary either. The emir rarely remained in

Kuwait during the summer months. Even so, the photographs of his departure, on top of the parliament suspension and the Mecca incident, gave the impression he just didn't care about Kuwait. The word in the street, and more particularly in the *diwaniyas* (men's gatherings), was dangerous for the monarchy. "The man is leaving again. He knows he's the king." I had mixed feelings. I wanted stability for my country and my family, but I also wanted freedom. My heart was not with the emir.

Events in Qatar, Bahrain, the UAE, and Oman mirrored those in Kuwait. The so-called democratic or near democratic systems in the Gulf were recognized for what they were—facades to protect and preserve the monarchies and central power conglomerates. Nothing had happened other than the failed attempt on Mecca, but fear spread, fueled by rumor.

I still had contacts with other members of parliament. Al-Hasawi, my old nemesis, phoned me to see what I knew. He was alarmed. "Yusef, what do you think? Are the Persians coming after us? I've heard there is an ISIL cell in Kuwait ready to strike. Tell me what you know. Should I get my family out?"

My only response was, "Summer is here. You have an excuse to get out." And I told him the truth. "I don't know anything more than I have already shared, but everything you say could be true."

The control of the press maintained by the governments began to fragment. In Bahrain the newspaper *Al-Wasat* spoke out against the king for the first time in anyone's memory. The sense of financial ease and peace that had existed in Kuwait, with interruption only during the Iraqi invasion of 1990, began to evaporate. Two major auto dealerships, Al-Bader and Al-Ghassan, advertised ridiculously low prices for their new vehicles. It looked like they were trying to dump their inventory and get out of business before it was too late.

Somehow my family remained at the center. The reasons for this phenomenon still were not clear to me. Perhaps it was due to the fact we were not Shia or Sunni but Christian. Perhaps it was the ironic and false protection of Mecca for which I was awarded credit. Or perhaps it was the statements I had made to Al Jazeera.

When Tahara rose on the morning of June 19 and turned on the faucet to brush her teeth, the pipes of our old house coughed, sputtered, and failed to produce water. We had large containers of drinking water in the refrigerator, but our supply was limited. We turned on the TV, and the news reporter was in front of the water desalinization plant where she announced that the system had failed for unknown reasons. The engineers were struggling to get the plant back on line. Tahara and I were particularly concerned for little Ephraim. We rushed out to the Sultan Center to buy water. By 8 a.m., there was already a line in front of the store, and one of the employees was in front of the building announcing that they were already sold out of water.

I phoned one of the men who used to work for my father as a herder. Latif was nearly eighty, but he was still active in the desert. "Latif, we need water. Can you help me get some for my family?" I drove home, exchanged the Mercedes for my Jeep, put several large canisters in the back, and picked up Latif at his home. He directed me to a water hole in the desert he knew would be full even in the summer, and we filled the canisters. At least something from my ancestors' time was still functional.

Back in Ahmadi I set about purifying the water for drinking. Pumping the water through a filter took several hours, and my forearms were aching, but finally I accumulated enough for several days. Still, the water tasted salty. My ancestors would not have needed the purification, but we were products of civilization. Thus, our lives were preserved through the old connections of my father, but for many the search for water was not so easy. Our loss of flowers was nothing compared to the difficulty many others experienced. My anger at the government grew. I saw our government for what it was: a tool in the hands of a few. "Rescue me, O my God, from the hand of the wicked, from the grasp of the unjust and cruel man" (Psalm 71:4).

Thus, the water riots of late June 2025 began. While the emir and much of his cabinet vacationed in London and Paris, not only the poor working class expatriates of Kuwait but also middle class Kuwaitis roamed the downtown streets at night in large groups. Windows were smashed at the Sultan Center down by the Gulf. The employees cowered while the rioters searched for bottled water. Finding none, they took all the soft drinks, milk cartons, and juice boxes instead. The police stood back and did nothing; in fact, several of them participated.

Bricks were thrown through the windows of several small stores in the Gold Souq, but no gold was taken. It was an act of outrage, not thievery. While the overall damage in the city was not widespread, the events marked a change in the attitude of Kuwaitis. The disobedience of the citizenry underlined new disrespect for the leadership.

The water disruption lasted eight days. The rumor spread that more than a 100 small children had died of dehydration, but the Minister of Information would not allow the government hospitals to release any information. My doctor friends in the state hospitals told me the child deaths from dehydration numbered less than five, but still the rumors escalated. Was ISIL responsible? The water flow was restored, and the riots stopped, but the damage was done to the public's confidence in the government.

On June 29 at 3 a.m., the air conditioning stopped. We were used to sleeping with the loud drone, and when the sound stopped, we soon awakened. The nighttime temperature outside was 90 degrees, and during the day reached 115. Power outages were common during the summer, but they usually lasted only a few hours. This one lasted five days, and the population, which had formerly existed there for centuries without air conditioning, exploded with anger. Some whispered that ISIL had sabotaged our power grid. The riots were repeated, and the newspaper showed a photo of the emir leaving a London spa.

On July 1, I spoke with Hibah in Doha where she faced similar challenges. She said, "Yusef, the country is in disarray. The people believe the government can no longer supply their needs effectively. And their needs of today are greater than yesterday."

Stories like these were heard throughout the Gulf. Some of the newspapers blamed the deficiencies on the falling price of oil, but oil had been fluctuating in a similar range for years. The United States gas and shale production had continued to rise too, displacing the need for the Middle Eastern product.

The real problem, I thought, was the inability of the Gulf's fake democracies to meet the needs of the people. The monarchies continued to twist and turn in the summer heat. All the while the emirs vacationed in cooler climes. Where were the funds that had formerly flowed toward solving such problems?

Another brushfire ignited on July 6, 2025. The Shias of Kuwait, nearly thirty percent of the population, still were not represented well by the news or state information systems. It was therefore a surprise when the commemoration of Ashura began. Such a celebration had not previously been a part of Kuwaiti culture; but now with the worsening governmental system and the increasing political awareness of minorities, Ashura took on a new significance. The sight of sweaty, bare-chested men marching down Gulf Road with swords and knives flashing in the bright sun formed a picture new to Kuwait. The police and military had no idea how to deal with a political, religious parade. They briefly attempted to terminate the marching by arresting twenty participants, but quickly recognized that their detention facilities would soon be overwhelmed. The event was allowed to run its course, and the day ended in some degree of peace.

But Kuwait had changed. The emir remained abroad until September. By the time he returned, the country considered him an uninvolved player. In earlier days his absence went unnoticed, but now it was the talk of the nation. Still there was no parliament to take action on the water or power shortage. The various ministers of state had apparently decided to remain out of Kuwait until the emir arrived to absorb most of the blame.

In the midst of all this confusion, I was summoned to Iran.

CHAPTER 13

EVENTS COALESCE

On August 1, I received a call from Karim Khadim in Tehran. "Yusef, you must come right away." Then, nothing but his heavy breathing on the line. There was no introduction, no *As-salaam alaikum,* no how are you, no real greeting of any kind.

I was silent for a moment, but recovered and replied, "No, I will not be coming."

"I'm not giving you a choice. There is too much I could say that would not be in your interest, or the interest of your family."

I went to Tahara who was nursing Ephraim in the garden. Even with the heat, she loved the morning sun, and the watering system moistened the air. "I won't let you go. Remember Yemen." She continued to look at Ephraim, and didn't make eye contact with me. "I thought you wouldn't come back then." Her refusal to look at me indicated she knew I was going anyway. I stood there with my hands on my hips, which she took it as a posture of defiance.

A tear rolled down Tahara's cheek. Of course, she was concerned about my going. This scenario was getting old for both of us—my going and her being left behind, uncertain if I would return and afraid. I answered, "If I refuse, there's no telling what

Khadim might unloose. Think of all I've done for the Persians, and he could share all of it." How much more ammunition would he need than the nuclear weapons, the transfer of funds from illegal sources, and the confusing business with the Yemenis? "If Khadim tells all he knows, it would be devastating to me—to all of us."

On August 3, I boarded Kuwait Airways Flight 54 to Tehran. The short flight landed at Imam Khomeini Airport thirty kilometers southwest of Tehran. Khadim met me in the terminal hall. I was surprised to see he was alone. His apparel was unusual too: yellow polo shirt, white slacks, and brown loafers. Was this a disguise of sorts? Certainly it was for him.

Out in the parking lot we could barely see the mountains beyond the city. The smog was up. He drove us back to Tehran in his black Lexus. He said little in the car other than pleasantries. The six-lane highway, the low, sandy hills, and the smog added to the tedium of the journey. I figured he still believed his car was bugged, and I joined his silence. When we finally arrived at the first destination, I was exhausted from waiting to know the reason for his summons.

We proceeded to dinner at a restaurant called Divan and sat down by one of the pillars across from the red, green, blue and white stained glass windows. Khadim ordered for me, the kabob *torsh* with leek rice. Torsh is a beef dish marinated in crushed walnuts, pomegranate juice, chopped parsley, olive oil and crushed garlic. I had heard Divan was the most expensive restaurant in the city, and the delicious dish softened me up.

With all these personal touches, I feared he was manipulating me. His skill in setting the stage for intrigue was unsurpassed as always. The first evening he didn't bring up anything of importance. He seemed anxious, often looking from side to side. I had enough experience with Iran to know the significance of potential government overseers, their omnipresence, and their devotion to duty. I appreciated there was no point in pushing him, but I was getting more and more upset at his slow approach.

After dinner he insisted on walking the streets of Tehran near the restaurant. It was at this point that I saw clearly that we were being watched. I saw a man in a short-billed leather cap and brown leather jacket, who I recognized from the airport, the restaurant, and now, here on the street.

As we walked the streets, I began to see even more differences from the Tehran of my previous experience. Several of the women made no attempt to cover their heads, and the police did not challenge them. We passed a small evangelical church that had opened in a storefront. It was Sunday night, and the church was noisy and full.

Khadim dropped me off at a small hotel in a poorer section of the city. I began to resent the mystery he was imposing upon me, and now felt annoyed by being relegated to a cheaper hotel. By the time I encountered the dirty sheets in my bed, I was fuming. Khadim's silence after bringing me all the way across the Gulf and this filthy hotel were infuriating. *Why had he demanded my presence here? Why was he "managing" me as he was? Was Khadim still an enemy? I did not know where he now stood.*

He met me the next morning for breakfast in a coffee shop near the hotel. He positioned himself out of view of the several monitoring cameras. *Why did the head of the Ministry of Economic Affairs and Finance need to be so careful?* Perhaps he needed money and planned to blackmail me. I was steaming with all his delays.

It turned out that my distrust and dislike of Khadim was misdirected. The times had changed, and so had Khadim.

He thanked me for coming to Tehran, and then he launched into his purpose. He was finally sincere. "Yusef, Iran is changing rapidly, more so than any of us would have expected. The imams are no longer able to enforce their leadership. The people want freedom, not only social and economic freedom, but also religious freedom. The theocracy is a shell with no substance." He shifted in his seat to check out the other patrons. "I'm sorry I couldn't get to the point sooner, but we've been followed much of the time, and they have advanced equipment." He was rigid in his seat and blinking rapidly.

"The vast wealth of the theocracy has been exposed and can no longer be concealed. The people know how much they've stolen from the nation's coffers. The government can't control all the blogs and tweets." For the first time, I saw that he was angry with his country's leadership, even though he had carried out the same policies. His face reddened and his upper lip showed sweat under his moustache. "Even those in the theocracy themselves see their authority as temporary. The intellectual vigor of the country can no longer be repressed. The people don't care about Israel or the bomb." I knew they never did.

By this time the coffee shop was emptying of its morning crowd. To remain inconspicuous, we walked to a park with many pine trees and towering plants and got lost among them. The morning had become pleasant for me, and my anger disappeared.

Khadim continued, "The main issue is that Christianity has spread with great speed. You know about the dreams. They've come to all classes of people. The old churches are full and the new churches are filling. The people have seen the results of the Salafist philosophy and ISIL, and they want no part of it." The Salafis, their doctrine originating in Egypt as a derivative of the strict, Sunni Wahhabi movement, were responsible for much of the cruelty and violence in ISIL Islam.

I nodded in agreement, but Khadim had not yet gotten to the point.

"Yusef, you wonder why I forced you to come. I've had a dream." I must have looked astonished. "Yes, I've had a dream. I'll not burden you with the content. I'm sure you can imagine. But a man I'd never seen before (or since) sat with me in a café. He explained what was happening to me in the dream. I've read the Bible, just as I've studied the Quran, and I have become a Christian. My family has followed me on this path, but we can't attend church or become openly Christian. My position won't allow it. If I stay in Tehran, sooner or later we'll be discovered. I must leave Iran. You must get me and my family to Kuwait. You must save us." Oh no, not another one on my doorstep. Afsin's

177

near disastrous slip was still on my mind. How could I deal with this much more prominent family?

I wanted to do nothing about his request, but just let him dangle on his own rope. After all he had done to me, involved me in the bomb debacle, I was full of his tricks and subterfuge. But I said, "Khadim, I will do my best." In my heart of hearts, Jesus' compassion came to the fore. I knew the struggle a Christian faced, and worse, the danger posed to their lives in Iran.

Khadim took me back to the airport and I booked a flight directly at the Kuwait Airways desk. I told him to wait for my call on his newly acquired burner cell phone, which I gave him as temporary and disposable method of communicating with me.

Once again the port in Bandar Bushehr would provide the best method of transfer for his family. The airport could not be used. I phoned Khadim with the instruction to drive his family to the port and board the Dolphin. Their passage across the northern Gulf at night was uneventful. The captain knew the routes of the Iranian gunboats and avoided them.

Upon arrival in Kuwait at the dock near the downtown Sultan Center, Khadim and his family looked like any other well-to-do family of Kuwaitis returning from a day of pleasure. We made as little as possible of their arrival. Getting all their bags (the family's possessions were ostentatious even by Kuwaiti standards) into the pickup was more conspicuous than we wanted, but it was accomplished within a few minutes. The onlookers dispersed, and we relaxed as we drove off. I took them to the Marriott and booked them in under the name Abdullah Al-Saleh. Khadim had already procured passports under that name, using his contacts in the Persian government.

Two days later *The Tehran Times* published a story about the mysterious disappearance of the head of the Ministry of Economic Affairs and Finance along with his entire family. "Foul play is suspected. Elements from ISIL are expected to claim responsibility." I few days later ISIL accommodated. They were eager to claim responsibility, even when they had done nothing, and so the transfer of Khadim and his family was accomplished with remarkable ease.

Unlike Afsin, Khadim's family needed little help integrating into the population. His Arabic was excellent, and he brought vast personal wealth with him in euros. He purchased the necessary documents for residency and a home in the Khalidiya neighborhood, and the family's name changed to Al-Qasar. By the next week they were attending Thawab's church.

###

In mid-September the emir quietly returned to Kuwait. Church members who worked at the airport told me he arrived at two in the morning and exited the plane alone directly into his limousine waiting on the tarmac. The leader attempted invisibility.

The parliament was still suspended from all action, and no elections were planned. When the emir summoned me to the palace on September 20, I had no idea why. The grounds of the palace were in disarray. The typically well-watered plants had died and not been replaced, apparently as a result of the disruption in water supply. The date palms were unkempt with many dead fronds. The dishdashas of the gate attendants were not freshly cleaned and pressed.

I was shown into his private quarters where visitors were never allowed. Country and western music was softly playing in the background. I had not heard Johnny Cash for a long time—not since London. Folsom Prison Blues, eh? The desk was piled with documents showing the stamps of several Gulf countries. The emir's chief of security had escorted me. He was dismissed.

"Yusef, thank you for coming." *I was not aware I had a choice.* "You know the state of affairs in Kuwait. I cannot convene the parliament or allow elections. The results would be unpredictable, and I cannot take that risk right now. This situation is far worse than you know." *But I did know.* "There are elements of the population who no longer want to be ruled by a monarch of any sort."

In fact, *no one wanted the monarchy* any longer. It had become, at best, irrelevant. I sat without responding. Emir Nawaf had aged years over the long summer.

He continued, "I must enumerate the obstacles so you will know what we're up against."

I could not fathom why he said *we*. I considered myself on the other side. The old man was taking advantage of me, just as he had done in the past. *Why me?* The emir was running over me to gain his last shred of advantage. "The plowers plowed upon my back; they made long their furrows" (Psalm 129:3). In truth, I was as angry as any of the others. I had been plowed long enough.

He went on, "The Shias are in complete revolt. For years they were no trouble. They were quiet, but now they are making themselves the focus. There are other dangerous elements in the country too. We know that ISIL is among us, waiting to strike. The Wahhabists here in Kuwait want Sharia law. We've been through that before. It's ridiculous, but the most dangerous group is the wealthy merchants. They want to be wealthier with no interference from the monarchy. I've asked you here because you don't represent any of these groups." I was the strangest bedfellow he could have chosen.

"You could say I represent the Christians in Kuwait."

"The Christians are no problem. They want only their strange God."

Finally, I spoke up, and the emir frowned, "What do you want of me?" My reasons for fearing the emir were decreasing.

"Yusef, you're one of the most respected men in Kuwait, perhaps the most respected. Who would have suspected that? I need your help in a personal way. I want you to host a half-hour TV show on all the networks twice weekly. The program will be *Yusef's Half Hour*. We will provide the script. You will discuss such topics as the history of Kuwait, showing how the emirs have wisely protected the state, the marvelous economy of Kuwait due to my benevolence, the generous provision of necessities for our population, the protection of personal freedoms, and other such important topics." So Nawaf's survival had been reduced to meaningless propaganda.

"Your Highness, I'm not sure I'm adequately prepared to present these ideas." Of all the crazy ideas I could have considered, this one was the strangest. Perhaps he had asked others and they had declined.

"As I have said, the material will be prepared for you. If you are considering not participating as I have directed, be aware there are those who could share more about your work in Iran. We understand your former supervisor, Karim Khadiim, is now missing, but we will find him in Tehran or somewhere else in the Gulf. Of that we are confident." The emir was still one not to be underestimated.

Who would tell the emir that Khadim was no longer Khadim, but now Qasar, an upper-class Christian living peacefully in Kuwait right under his nose? I would never tell him that because the emir's security men could find him and force him to talk.

The emir dismissed me from his quarters. An Indian assistant arranged the TV show times as I left out of the palace. I returned to my wife to tell her what it had been all about.

Tahara said, "You have no choice but to do as the emir asks. He's right in one thing: You are the most respected man in Kuwait." She took Ephraim in her arms and went into the garden to be alone with him. I needed her support, but Ephraim soaked up all her attention, and for a moment I was jealous of him.

I was unraveled by the emir's order and my lack of ability to refuse it. My anger increased because Tahara saw my weakness. I thought of Kuwait as my Babylon. "O daughter of Babylon, doomed to be destroyed, blessed shall he be who repays you with what you have done to us!" (Psalm 137:8). I wished I could repay, and while I did not want Kuwait to be destroyed, I began to pray more fervently for changes in my country. *Was God increasing my faith still more?*

On Tuesday evening I reported to the state-run TV network where the broadcast would be taped. The other networks in the city were required to carry the show. I came in a sport coat and trousers, but they made me change into a white gutra and dish-dasha instead. I needed to look Kuwaiti. Then came the makeup; its odd smell made me sick. They took a while matching my skin tone. I had hoped to see the text of my broadcast prior to going in front of the camera, but there was no script. I was expected to read a teleprompter.

The first evening's program was a reasonably accurate rendition of the history of Kuwait from the late nineteenth century to the middle of the twentieth century leading up to Kuwait's independence from the British in 1961. The overall emphasis was on the wise choices made by the Al-Sabah family, beginning with the great Mubarak (the murderer of his two brothers) himself.

The second evening, on the other hand, was a completely inaccurate interpretation of the generosity of the Al-Sabahs in general and, in particular, the current emir, Nawaf Al-Ahmad Al-Jaber Al-Sabah. I read the lies and tried to keep from choking on them.

When I arrived home, Tahara restrained herself, for which I was grateful. She brought out a dish of my favorite chocolate ice cream. She left off mentioning the TV debacle and went straight to Ephraim's latest trick—his gurgling laughter when she made faces at him.

The subject matter for the show continued to deteriorate from that time on. When I learned the next program was to deal with the protection of personal freedoms, I feigned illness and skipped the show. My sick day was not well received by the emir. A messenger arrived with flowers and a note at our home, "Dear Yusef, I am very sorry you are ill. I pray for the continued health of your family. Nawaf." *Continued health of my family? I got that message loud and clear.* Behind those sugary words was a threat: do what I tell you or your family will get it. I discarded the note before Tahara could see it.

For the third program on personal freedoms, which I could not avoid, I resolved to use the opportunity to my advantage. I read the teleprompter with the first few platitudes, such as: "The Kuwait people are free to travel wherever they wish" and "the emir and his cabinet encourage the expression of statements conducive to the harmony of our state."

Then I stopped reading the teleprompter and continued on my own. "The emir has told me that laws prohibiting criticism of the royal family will no longer be enforced, and the laws against apostasy will no longer be enforced either." Last of all, I added, "He has declared that one's religion can be freely practiced in Kuwait. Kuwaiti Christian churches are encouraged to open their doors."

By this time, the crew and director were all fumbling madly with the script, searching for the correct text. Then they recovered their senses, shut down the teleprompter, concluded my program, and picked up with "special news" by the regular newsman. Then they showed a week old video of the emir and his staff greeting a delegation from Oman, a crowd of white flowing robes. The video was repeated twice with different narrative to fill the time.

I drove back to Ahmadi. Tahara was at the door to greet me with tears flowing down her cheeks and little Ephraim in her arms. "Yusef, we'll be killed, and no one will know what happened to us."

My explosive comments had taken away the courage of my beautiful wife. Her response made me even angrier with the emir and his collaborators. "Deliver me, O Lord, from evil men; preserve me from violent men, who plan evil things in their heart and stir up wars continually" (Psalm 140:1-2). I needed to be rescued. What had I done? I had taken a huge risk, but it was not just my personal risk. In my pride to do some great and tricky thing, I had put my entire family in danger. Was there something I could do to fix this? Was this in the Lord's hands or mine?

By the next morning we were expecting the worst, but the day was quiet. Then, on the morning of the second day, we were greeted by a report in *The Kuwait Times* on my last program. The article was titled, "Support for Emir Grows." The paper detailed my remarks and concluded with the community's response. Al-Husseini was one of those quoted. "The emir has demonstrated that his thinking reflects the will of the people."

The TV showed video from a well-to-do diwaniya with several prominent citizens praising the broadmindedness of the new policies. They were particularly pleased that their criticisms of the emir would no longer be considered treason. A small group from our church paraded in front of the palace with placards of thanks to the emir.

Many took the announcement of the new freedoms as a loosening of the grip held by the monarchy, a move the majority was happy to see. The emir was now committed to my statements by events he had unintentionally set in motion. It looked like he had handed us a victory with his little TV show, and I saw no way he could retract the new policies I had foisted upon him.

But the new "rules" were a danger for the emir in other portions of the community. The Islamists, and there were more than a few, were shocked at the new liberality, so the emir now had to deal with another enemy. Would this menace fall on my family as well? It was becoming too complicated to grasp the Big Picture. My thoughts were only man-sized.

The most obvious result was the rapid proliferation of Kuwaiti Christian churches, or rather their surfacing from the shadows. One opened in a large home church down the street from us in Ahmadi. On the following Friday, there were no parking places on our street.

Events were spinning faster and faster. No more accusations of apostasy? Really? Such allegations were almost a sport in some sections of the Islamic community. Freedom for the opening of

Christian churches for Kuwaiti citizens? The prohibition of new churches had been a standard in the community, and the fact of its reversal was a shock to all Muslims. How could this be stopped without making more news? The emir's little TV program had backfired into areas unanticipated.

Yet there were still no codified legal protections, and the status of Christians was as fragile as the morning dew. The system was in disarray.

I didn't hear from the emir for several weeks. In those weeks, the news of upheavals in the community got worse, as if that were possible. I kept expecting to hear from the palace, but there was nothing. When the next call finally came, it was a prelude to another potential disaster.

CHAPTER 14

THE EMIR SCRAMBLES

The upturn in opinion concerning the monarchy was brief. In mid-October, following another lengthy and unexplained disruption of power and water, citizen morale in Kuwait plummeted. Kuwaitis filled the streets, joined by the ever-present Third World expatriates, and roamed the area around the Kuwait stock exchange extending up to Ahmed Al Jaber Street. The demonstrations were peaceful and not organized. Street vendors were out *en masse* with their beef or lamb sharmas. Several cart drivers with signs saying, "Water Not Supplied by Emir," sold bottled water.

Traffic was delayed. Those in the traffic jam refrained from honking out of respect for the protestors. The police smiled, waved at the demonstrators, and did not interfere. Some later joined them. Altogether, it was an expression of community unity against the government, and the peace of Kuwait reigned among the newly freed citizenry.

The news from the other Gulf monarchies was not good, and confidence in the leadership of the emirate system eroded. The initial reasons had been fear of Iran and the Shia on one side and ISIL on the other, and while I could not see any connection at this juncture, I wondered if the People of the Return were behind the disorder? It was as if the Shia had a direct line to Al Jazeera in promulgating news of their potential for civil disruption. And now there was the added burden of deficits in the delivery of community services. Only the government could be blamed for these.

However, the most dramatic disturbance was yet to come, and it had nothing to do with the Shia. The emir had been siphoning off oil funds for years; most Kuwaitis had accepted the probability of this theft. The fact that the diversion of funds was not proven allowed a layer of fantasy to buffer it.

On November 1, Al Jazeera broke a story in the international press about the emir's theft of oil funds, and it centered first in Kuwait. At first, this was a rehash of old themes, but soon the story became accepted as truth.

For a brief time before his earlier deportation, Esau had been involved in these transfers. Although the law required transfer of oil income funds to the state treasury, five percent had been sent to the emir's offshore accounts. This illegal transfer had been discovered and was well documented, no longer just a rumor. The Kuwaiti gossip line spread details of the story and embellished those details. As the story traveled around the community, the amount of money stolen from their nation grew with each repetition.

Abdullah Al-Bader invited me to an upper class *diwaniya*. I was uncertain of the reason for the invitation, because they were not usually open to Christians, but it was immediately apparent that he wanted me to act as disseminator of detailed information about the emir's actions. I was trapped again, but I had to admit that I was becoming enamored with all the attention and the thought of my advancing role.

The attendees entered the brightly lit rectangular hall and shed their sandals at the door. The home had been constructed with a magnificent, gold-trimmed, elongated diwaniya room. The men settled into their traditional positions on the floor and folded their legs under themselves on the big cushions. Normally these meetings began slowly and in a disorganized fashion. Important remarks were usually delayed until after everyone had arrived, and tea had been served; but this discussion began early and in earnest. Everyone had come on time to hear the important versions of the news.

The rant about the Al Jazeera story began almost immediately. In past years their remarks would have met the standard for treason. My host, Saleh Al-Ghaniim, and Hassan Al-Kharafi fanned each other's flames. Their intensity frightened me. *Did this mean we were headed for violence against the royal family? I wanted no part of that.* Arab verbal harangues often exceeded any intended violence. I hoped that was the case.

Al-Bader started off. "That thief of an emir has robbed us blind. He's taken a huge portion of our country's oil wealth for himself." It was early in the evening and already we were off to get the noose. A young Indian *farash* (or male servant) had just delivered the tea.

Al-Ghaniam jumped in. "It's been going on for years. How

could we not have known? How were we so stupid? The men of his family have always been in the same game. The total amount is incalculable. They've avoided detection by sending the money to their private accounts outside Kuwait." The rise in the level of anger in the group astounded me. There were grunts of agreement with each statement.

Al-Karafi clarified the details for the rest of the diwaniya. He was the financial expert, and he spoke with precision. "Here's the bottom line: A fixed percentage of oil revenue is designated by law to flow into the government treasury, but a significant portion of these funds have been transferred without bank oversight. The funds never showed up on government ledgers. This practice has become routine, unknown, and undetectable by the usual accounting procedures that the Sabahs set in place. The whole thing has been beautifully planned and executed. The thief has no honor, only the skill to deceive." As he spoke, the veins on his forehead bulged. He was so excited that little particles of saliva erupted from his mouth when he spoke.

Al-Bader wanted to make sure the group understood the magnitude of the theft. "As of November 1, 2025, the total value of the assets of the State of Kuwait were 300 billion Kuwaiti dinars. At the exchange rate of 3.5 dollars per dinar, this amount was over one trillion dollars, which would certainly seem adequate to fund and protect our small country. Reality is that we should have more than twice as much as that." He shook his tea glass with a quick back and forth motion, which indicated he wanted no more, and put the glass on the farash's silver tray with an audible clang. The young man's eyes got big.

Al-Ghaniam blasted away. "Bloggers have revealed that the amount in the emir's private accounts exceeds 500 billion dinars, much more than what is in the Kuwait treasury. He is the prince of thieves." The diwaniya was the most effective news source for the wealthy citizens of Kuwait. It was also the base for the advice and consent authority they gave to support the emir. Consent had now been withdrawn in any practical sense. At that moment I knew it was over for the emir. He could still preserve his life if he acted quickly. I was in this more deeply than I thought. Any sense of enjoyment ended.

The meeting went on like that for three hours. The conversation remained on the subject of the emir's embezzlement of funds, and didn't ramble in the usual manner. I had to sit there and take it all in. In contrast to the way the evening ended in normal times with slow, individual departures, everyone got up and departed at the same time. I was drained with the diatribes. *What was my role in this revolt? No one had asked me anything and I had not spoken. Once again, I found myself confused. What was next?*

Esau was the focus of scandal again, even though he remained out of Kuwait for many years. The current emir had used him as transfer agent on many occasions, and it was now clear Esau sill had a role. He had been caught before, and now he was caught again. In all this intrigue, the United States had avoided getting involved in the mess. The American Department of Justice wanted to remain aloof from Kuwaiti internal matters. The emir's staff leaked information to the papers, and it was reported, not entirely accurately, that Esau had been at the center of the fund transfer for many years. While there was some truth to the allegation, the transfers had been in progress for much longer than Esau's tenure. The emir was trying to duck.

However, it also came out that even after the spectacular TV footage of Esau's earlier banishment from Kuwait, the man had been quietly allowed back into Kuwait by the emir. The reason became clear: The aging emir had needed him for the last few, essential financial transfers, transfers that were all the more vital in the coming fiasco.

Once again the emir tried in vain to set up Esau as the culprit. In an attempt to regain control of the situation, Esau once more became the fall guy. The poor man had been invited back only to demonstrate his criminality. He was taken by security forces with cameras everywhere, taken to the airport, placed on a flight to New York, and summarily deported again. He had the haggard look of a trapped thief, and his aging demeanor added to his desperation. The Al-Tamimi family watched this televised spectacle with some degree of satisfaction. At least this little this spectacle made us feel better, but how could they use Esau twice in this manner?

The emir then went on TV, where he delivered a most unusual speech. Until this time, the emir had never bothered to explain anything to the citizens. "My fellow Kuwaitis, I must sadly report we had a thief among us, one Esau Allison. Unbeknownst to me, he had been systematically stealing funds from our oil revenues. He has carried out this procedure for many years and taken much. Although we beneficently and with forgiveness allowed him back into Kuwait once, I can report to you now that he has now been deported and the matter is brought to a close." The emir thus made it seem that Esau was the thief and not he, himself. He made his best attempt to explain the situation and shift the blame, but the fact that Esau could not have done this without the emir's approval was obvious to all, so Nawaf's explanation failed.

Since Esau was still an American citizen, Nawaf said Kuwait didn't want to get involved in his prosecution. A local trial would have been the proper way of handling the situation, but his immediate deportation avoided his testimony. Suddenly, and with no action on our part, we were at least rid of at least one derelict enemy, and for the second time.

The emir's diversion worked only briefly. It was not enough. The Kuwaiti local news systems, even those under direct state control, were compelled to report the longstanding diversion of funds. In the end, Esau Allison was not as newsworthy as the emir. The accounts on Kuwaiti TV were bland, but direct and accurate: "Al Jazeera has reported the misuse of Kuwait funds for the personal benefit of the emir and his family over a very long period of time." They did not yet use the word *theft*. The stations, for their own protection, quoted Al Jazeera rather than making the report their own.

That the theft of Kuwaiti resources had occurred for so long with such regularity and so systematically was especially infuriating to Kuwaitis who were wealthy. They could have been even richer. And to those of lesser means, who had suffered at the hands of the often less-than-adequate state medical system, the occurrence was beyond infuriating. Every child or parent who had died in Kuwait-run hospitals was suddenly the victim of the theft. The enemy was now clear. Believers could legitimately call down God's wrath. I joined in. "Bow your heavens, O Lord, and come down! Touch the mountains so that they smoke! Flash forth the lightning and scatter them: send out your arrows and rout them!" (Psalm 144:5-6).

But the real threat to the monarchy came from the merchant families. Without their support, the emir could not maintain a consensus of leadership. I was summoned to the palace to meet with him, along with the merchant families. *Why was I included?* The Al-Tamimis were rich, but not part of the preeminent merchant class. By now, I had learned to simply go, so I went without question.

The emir's main assistant first took me into one of the smaller rooms off the main corridor. He said, "The emir is expecting you to assist with the merchants. If you are there, they will have more trust. They respect you and what you have done for the state."

"But what can I say? The information in the news sounds correct." Would I have to bear some sort of dual role? As always, I was dragged along by circumstance. *Was this the Lord's intervention? Possibly. I needed to be aware of the leading of the Holy Spirit in this meeting.*

The sad assistant had no response to my question.

When I entered the emir's receiving area with the merchants, I found more of them there than I anticipated. Although their number was only fifteen, the power and influence they wielded was immense. The usual greetings were curtailed, and there were no smiles among the merchants. Neither the merchants nor the emir were eager to initiate the conversation, and they looked to me. I broke the unpleasant silence. "To the praise of Allah, we must preserve the peace and harmony of Kuwait. How can I help you in this noble aim?" I immediately realized my remark was foolish and too simpleminded for the situation. Harmony had disappeared. I looked around the room for others to jump in, but their faces were impassive.

The emir was silent. We sat quietly on the gold brocaded couches, waiting for the voice of a senior member. Abu Salim Al-Bader, the oldest of the group, spoke next. "We're here because our confidence in the longstanding model of Kuwait leadership is tarnished. Perhaps it can never be polished again. We want consider alternatives, and consider them vigorously." I was reminded of the events in the palace of the Qatari emir.

The emir shot back, "Alternatives to leadership? In the name of Allah, what are you suggesting?" The matter of his theft of state funds had not been mentioned in terms clear enough for him. *How could it be that Nawaf still didn't get it? He was very old, possibly nearing ninety, but was he so old that he did not understand the issues surrounding him now?*

Al-Kharafi spoke next, "First, the money must be returned. Then we can talk about leadership alternatives."

The emir rose and with a nod dismissed the group. His response was much harsher than anyone anticipated, and the state of affairs moved ever closer to cataclysm.

As we departed the palace, Al-Bader pulled me aside. "Your brother, Binyamin, has been working with us. We've long suspected such a diversion of funds has been occurring, but we couldn't find the documentation. Binyamin uncovered the trail and followed it from the sources to where they are held now. This has not just been the practice of the present emir; this has been going for years. We think it may be true of all the Gulf monarchies. The Saudi kings made no pretense. They just took the money for their families, but never mind. That one—bin Salman—he's something. He makes no apologies, but the monarchs on our side of the Gulf have pretended otherwise. We must have a new government. It will be better for all if the change is voluntary. You must tell the emir." *How had all this become mine to do? On one hand, I was enthralled with my involvement, but I still feared the result of such a confrontation and my responsibility in it.*

The merchants felt they had lost money important to them. Others with far less had not knowingly experienced the loss as yet. I was indignant over the ironies of the moment. How strange it was that we all emerged feeling that we had been robbed, and then we drove off in our expensive cars.

But embezzlement of the riches of Kuwait could not be kept

secret, even with the emir's nearly complete control of the local news. Tahara made certain Al Jazeera picked up every news strand, in spite of her fears for our family. It was the principle of the thing. She arranged an interview with Binyamin, and once again the Al-Tamimis made the news. The interview took place in our living room. The Al Jazeera news woman was delighted with the opportunity to make international news. Young Binyamin made a dapper appearance in his red-and-white checkered gutra and white dishdasha. He was so young and handsome. "Kuwait has been tricked and lied to. There has never been a theft on this scale. The sheer magnitude of it exceeds all other thefts in world history." The hyperbole, if it was hyperbole, made a great opening line. When he was asked how he had discovered the theft, he replied. "The merchants suspected that all the oil income was not accounted for, so they employed me to make a search. My investigation began with the oil companies and ended with finding the accounts in the Cayman Island banking system." The interviewer looked very pleased with her work. Was there an Arab alternative to the Pulitzer?

CNN and Fox picked up the story and repeated it with their usual, pointless frequency. Interesting how CNN gave it a liberal slant, while Fox meted out the conservative bent, all on the same material.

And still the theme was not complete. Merchants in Qatar, Bahrain, UAE and Oman contacted Binyamin. The investigations of their systems required two months, but by January the findings were clear. The same pattern of abuse was present in all the monarchies. It was as if the emirs had collaborated in their methodology, and each one of them had done it for years. These findings, in combination with abuses of various other types—religious, social, and political—set the stage for near governmental breakdowns in their little Gulf states.

The amounts of the embezzlements were huge. The erosion of trust in the governments multiplied, and any path back to the old ways seemed hopeless. In Bahrain violent riots broke out in the streets, and police overreacted with live ammunition. Five demonstrators were killed while the cameras rolled. In Qatar the emir ordered a crackdown and curfew in advance of riots, but the public reaction was only strengthened by those measures. In comparison to the outcry in the other countries, the one in Kuwait was modest.

The Gulf was no longer at peace with itself, and the rulers had no way to defend themselves or further obscure what had formerly remained hidden. The Shia, who had known for some time they were second- or third-class citizens, reveled in their newfound power. Some of these were the People of the Return. *How did this continue to haunt me? And why? I saw now that God had placed me in this muddle.*

On January 5, 2026, I was again summoned to the emir's palace.

I entered the palace, but was not taken to the reception area; rather, the attendant led me to the private quarters. This signaled a significant shift. When I entered the room, the emir was seated with his arm stretched out over the back of the gold cloth couch. He didn't rise or smile at me. He was bareheaded and wearing a wrinkled dishdasha. His shiny, bald head reflected the bright lights of the room. For a long moment he did not look up, and he spoke quietly, not with authority, "Yusef, you came. I wasn't sure you would."

The fact that the emir no longer considered his summons binding startled me. He motioned for me to sit. "I don't know if even you can preserve the monarchy. The merchants have garnered further support. I dare not call for elections. There is talk of a new constitution. I must ask you to go to Doha next week. The Gulf Cooperation Council (GCC) will convene, and I need you to represent me. This meeting is the yearly one where the heads of the Gulf States normally attend. I've talked with the others and none of us will attend except for the Saudi king. If we leave our states, we could be deposed by a coup."

Since the boycott of Qatar by Saudi Arabia, Bahrain, and UAE, the GCC had fallen into disrepair, and its function had declined to the point of a forgotten formality, but these new concerns about theft among the Gulf rulers had transformed the GCC again into a necessity.

"Certainly I will go. But what is the point of the meeting right now?" The arrows kept coming. Indeed, why now?

"The meeting is a subterfuge. The emirs feel we must appear to be taking some sort of action to lessen the impact of the situation.

We're trying to avoid disaster by making a show of our accomplishments. Perhaps some new superficial, harmless freedoms will satisfy the people. Please think of some."

I saw the sad and discouraged emir as a sign of real change. For the first time, I acknowledged God working. I had known this in a small way, but I now saw His hand was present. As always, God spoke to me in a psalm. For years the psalms of my mother had both challenged and echoed my inner feelings. First, there were the songs of lament, complaining to God. Then, more recently, the psalms expressing my anger over ongoing events. The liberation of my anger now gave way to praise. "O Lord, our Lord, how majestic is your name in all the earth! You have set your glory above the heavens. Out of the mouth of babies and infants, you have established strength because of your foes, to still the enemy and the avenger" (Psalm 8:1-2). I saw how God had asserted control, and real faith rose within me, a gift of God Himself.

As an emissary of the emir, I flew in his private plane to Doha, landing at the Hamad International Airport. The attendants treated me as I imagined the emir himself was treated. When the plane came to rest and the door opened, a large white Cadillac met me on the tarmac and took me to the Marsa Malaz Kempinski Hotel on the Pearl where the meeting was to be held. The room reserved for me was the emir's suite with flowers, fruit, and a liquor cabinet. The paperwork on the desk indicated I was to set the agenda of the meeting for the following morning. I called Hibah and Tahara to fill them in on events and ask their advice.

Hibah knew all about the rapid, overtaking events. "Yusef, this time was set by God for you. You must do what's right for the people of the Gulf, and for the believers in the Gulf. In Qatar the gospel has spread without restraint. The emir here has virtually been destroyed by the discoveries of Binyamin and the merchants. He has no resources to curtail the movements of the Spirit. The time our mother looked to, prayed for, is now. You must craft the agenda to coincide with the Spirit that leads you." She assumed the Spirit led me. I wished I were as certain as she. I prayed and asked God to do exactly that.

Tahara was still fearful. She cried and said, "I want you home with me. I know you're in danger. Ephraim and I are in danger. The emir still has those who are for him. You must relieve him and the others of their position. That's the only way. You've got to bring this to an end, and do it quickly." Her level of emotion was higher than I had heard before. I was lost about how to fix things. The woman I loved was distressed with me for not being stronger, or so I felt. I couldn't defend her and Ephraim to the extent she deserved. *Could I leave their defense to God?*

I had to respond with more courage than I possessed. "Tahara, God will preserve us. He hasn't put all this in motion to see it end before its conclusion. I'm confident His hand is on this mission." I surprised myself with this revelation. In saying this, I came closer to believing it.

The blank agenda and computer screen loomed before me. First, we needed a report from the GCC countries about their local conditions in regard to the level of disruption they were experiencing. Second, we needed to know if each state government still functioned in supplying the needs of the population. Third, what could be done to repair the rift? Fourth, could the money be returned? And finally, and perhaps the most delicate matter, what would happen to the Shias? Would the group that was gathering even be interested in their fate? There was more I couldn't even consider.

We convened at nine the next morning in the Venezia Ballroom, which was much too spacious for the group of twelve Gulf representatives present. We had trouble with the microphone system but after all the participants were audible, I called us to order, feeling entirely out of place in this role. I asked if there were any objections to the agenda and my proceeding as moderator. The Omani representative, the one female of our group, laughed and said, "How can we refuse the savior of Mecca?" Even Bin Salman, sitting apart from the others, couldn't object.

One by one, the representatives of Qatar, Oman, Bahrain, and the seven men from the separate UAE States all stated that their emirs no longer had the trust of the people; and that, consequently, public disorder was present and increasing.

I felt particularly sorry for the Omanis. The Sultan Qaboos was an Ibadi, really an outsider. The Ibadi branch of Islam broke off long before the Sunni-Shia schism. They followed the Quran too, but did not believe in imams belonging to the lineage of the Prophet. Instead being an imam was a question of piety to which anyone could attain if led to do so. They were tolerant toward other faiths, but not toward dissent in their country. Qaboos was the only non-Sunni among the Gulf leadership of twelve. His association with the Sunni leaders in the council had dragged him into the same category; but on the other hand, he was guilty of identical financial indiscretions.

Mohammed Bin Salman of Saudi Arabia was the only true country leader present. Bin Salman sat with arms folded, chin elevated, avoiding eye contact with all. Why should he engage? Why was he even there? While his kingdom's management of funds was practically identical to that of the other States, it was an accepted reality in his country.

The second question about the needs of the people turned out to be confusing. Compared to the rest of the world, the citizens of the Gulf lived a privileged existence. Therefore their perceived needs far exceeded what others deemed reasonable. But when it was considered what the money taken by the emirs could have purchased—better education, better health care, and the like—the populations of each country were inconsolable and demanding change.

The third question posed to the group, the possibility of a solution, brought similar negative responses. The Qatari representative became incensed, "These emirs, these thieves, must leave us."

The Bahraini envoy added, "Yes, the emirs must leave but what will we have left? If we have parliaments, they won't know how to function without a monarch. We have no experience in doing that."

We stopped for lunch, which consisted of grilled hamour and leg of lamb. The quality of the food seemed proper for monarchs.

I couldn't eat. I skipped the meal and phoned Hibah to inform her of the lack of progress. I was concerned about her because of her marriage into the Qatari royal family. She replied, "Fareed has cut ties with the emir as much as possible. The fact we're Christians has made that split easier. The emir is gathering his personal entourage and his many possessions, and I think they're preparing to leave the country."

After lunch, as a solution, I suggested the emirs might simply agree to return the money to the state treasuries. Bin Salman, who had said little the entire morning, laughed aloud. His cackling only accentuated his isolation from the group. There was agreement, however, among the others that returning the money would go a long way toward repairing the damage. Various public works projects could be immediately begun. The Omani woman added, "The money could be distributed among the population. The amount per citizen would be between one and two hundred thousand dollars. Large families would get millions." The enthusiasm among the group rose on that note.

The meeting closed early in the afternoon of the first day. We would all return home and propose a return of the embezzled funds to the emirs. Given the sensitivity of the Shia issue, I deleted that topic. The day had been short, but I was worn out. *Should any more disasters be introduced?*

As I began to close the meeting, the Qatari representative moved that I be elected Secretary General of the Gulf Cooperation Council. I responded, "Thank you for the honor, but I'm not sure of the legality of the appointment in view of the absence of the emirs."

I didn't want the job. The psalms failed me at that moment. Or, rather, I failed the psalms.

He responded, "Never mind that; we're far beyond such a consideration. The legality of our position is whatever we establish." The vote was unanimously in my favor. I later learned Fareed had instigated the move.

Al Jazeera promptly ran the story that I was now the Secretary General of the Gulf Cooperation Council. In an editorial, they raised the question about the possible new significance of the office if there were no emirs in the Gulf except for the Saudi leader. I discovered Hibah had written the piece.

As I left the hotel, I marveled at the odd course of events, and at how little control I had to direct their path. God was indeed in charge. Right there in the street, just before entering the limousine, I looked up to heaven and lifted my arms in praise to God. Those in the car park stared at me as I spoke out the words of the psalm. "Lift up your heads, O gates! And be lifted up, O ancient doors, that the King of glory may come in. Who is this King of glory? The Lord, strong and mighty, the Lord, mighty in battle! (Psalm 24:7-8).

Throughout the Gulf, the emirs tried various routes to stave off the crisis. The Omani sultan and the Bahrain emir declared martial law and arrested those who spoke against them. Nawaf in Kuwait announced that each nuclear family would receive 25,000 dinars as a supplement to their income. Such payments had been given out in the past at critical times. The amount, however, was far too small to satisfy the wealthy merchants, and they were the only ones who really counted.

On January 13, I returned to see the emir. I was startled when I arrived at the palace. The fleet of vehicles normally present had been reduced to three. In the great hallway, the paintings were gone. The emir met me, unsmiling, which was now his default expression.

"Your Highness, I may have a solution for you. The council has offered a possible way to repair the damage. You could return all the funds in your private account to the state treasury and cease the diversion of funds in the future."

It seemed that he had already considered such an option. "Yusef, I thank you again for your service. I will not return the funds. I've talked with all the others. None of us will return the funds. What is the point of being an emir if we can't take what we want? Emirs do not yield. They rule."

"I don't know what else to say. I can't predict the consequences for you here then. There are many complications besides the money."

" 'In shā' Allāh," and he dismissed me. *Was I, as the Secretary General of the Gulf Cooperation Council, to be his executioner, his prosecutor, or his next victim? I had no idea.*

Then the decisive news broke. Once again Binyamin was the silent hero. He immediately released his information to Al Jazeera. The headline read, "US and Great Britain Buy Gulf Emirs." The story revealed that for fifteen years the two great powers had made secret transfers of money to the Gulf emirs. The emirs had essentially been paid off as a reward for preventing their countries from developing democracies. In looking back at the history of the Gulf States, one could see many instances when the emirs had disbanded parliaments. It was now evident that American and British funds had been used to support these endeavors by paying off critical political players in the various Gulf States. The United States and Britain knew it would be easier to control the emirs than any fledgling Arab democracies. Any shred of credibility the emirs possessed was thereby destroyed. It could not be determined how much money had been given to them, but the amount must have been immense. Britain and America had been considered culprits and interferers for years, so there was nothing new there. All the blame fell on the emirs.

On the other side of the Gulf in Iran, events were less well publicized but cataclysmic nevertheless. And the source of the calamity had originated in little Kuwait.

CHAPTER 15

THE ULAMA ATTACK

Karim Al-Qasar, formerly Karim Khadim, phoned me shortly after my arrival back in Kuwait. "Yusef, you must come to my home." Another demand I couldn't refuse. He would not have made such a request without a good reason. At four o'clock, I arrived at their new and generous home in Khalidiya on Tripoli Street. The two-story home with its four large columns in front was well kept and the smallest dwelling in a neighborhood of larger homes. Karim had been careful to avoid ostentation by Kuwaiti standards. I saw no servants, an oddity for the area. I parked under the palm tree on the circular red brick driveway avoiding the active sprinklers.

He met me at the door himself, took me into the study, and shut the door. The bookshelves were still nearly empty, but we stepped onto one of the finest carpets I had ever seen, outstanding in its stitching, complexity of design, and variety of colors. "I'm afraid they're looking for me. I've given much information to the lower level Persian *ulama* (religious leaders) about the financial goings-on of the Ayatollah and his cronies in Tehran. Perhaps that was unwise, but it's done. These white knights are going after the Supreme Leader. I've made them aware of the funds he's taken from the country. It's just like Kuwait. Ali Khameini is an old man now, but he won't surrender what he has."

He paced about the study on the expensive carpet, holding his hands clasped behind his back, his fingers in constant motion. His wife opened the door to bring us tea. He didn't speak to her. She put the tray down and left without his acknowledgement. Either he was being discourteous, or he didn't want to involve her, and I figured it was probably the latter. Khadim continued. He walked in circles around the study, reflecting his distress. "There is a small but vigorous group of five theocrats with the Ayatollah who are also benefitting from the money. The *ulama* of lesser rank are the problem for him. They tell me they're going to announce the embezzlement. If Khameini believes I'm responsible for telling the *ulama*, he'll send his men after me. He'll find my family and me. I know he can do it. You must go to Tehran and talk with President Mohammad Zarif. The theocracy is crumbling. Zarif may be the man to save Persia. Now is the time for this desperate move. Yusef, please protect my family. I'm begging you."

Zarif had won the support of the people following his negotiation of the nuclear treaty ten years earlier. Iran had prospered with the resulting infusion of funds, but to a lesser degree than expected. Was Zarif the one who could take his country back from the theocracy? What I heard from Karim seemed unlikely to me, beyond anything I thought possible for Iran.

I tried to make excuses. "But I have no real interest in Iran. I don't even understand the politics there, so what's the point of me going? Why would Zarif even agree to see me?" As soon as I said it, I realized how ridiculous that statement was. I was an expert in Persian politics by default, which was no secret. But I couldn't take any more of this: first, Secretary General of the Gulf Council and now meddling in Iranian affairs of state.

Karim pressed the subject. He was bursting with his need for me to act in his behalf. And in a real way, I was responsible for him. "You have every interest in Iran. You know of all the dreams, all the Jesus stories. The number of believers there is now immense. Zarif knows this. He'll be the winner, and he needs to know you're with him. I don't want to point this out to you, but I will. You have no choice. You're in too deep." Neither of us touched the tea, and by this time it was too cold to drink.

"Whether I'm with him or not, what difference would it make?"

"You still don't get it do you? You're going to be the leader of the Gulf. Sooner or later, you'll have to acknowledge it."

The dream of my childhood, at my fifth birthday, came roaring back to my mind. In the dream I had seen myself as the king of the whole Gulf. My family had dismissed the episode as a fantasy, and convinced me to do the same. But now? Now, the dream was taking shape right before my eyes! It had become a reality; and more than that, I had to submit to God's will. The fact that I might be His instrument in this great change in the Gulf required me to accept the faith God extended to me.

Karim had asked for my help to secure his safety and that of his family. He knew everything about me there was to tell. He was right. I had no choice. I had a destiny to fulfil and I knew it.

"I'll go see Zarif." As I left the home, his wife stood in the other room and watched me depart through the teak double doors with the gold-tinted knobs. Now I had to go tell Tahara.

Once again Tahara was distraught. Knowing I would return to Tehran broke her heart again. "Yusef, surely they'll keep you this time." I had put her through too much. She had come to me as a beautiful, courageous reporter, and now she was a mother, watching her child's father and beloved husband go off to war (or at least its political equivalent)—again.

I informed the emir I would go to Iran. I handled the matter by phone. Every time I entered the palace, I came away more discouraged, so I avoided the trip. After my going through two secretaries, Nawaf finally came on the line. His response was more enthusiastic than I anticipated. "Yes, certainly, I'll support you. It's the kind of news I need. You'll be the envoy of Kuwait seeking to heal the Shia problem in the Gulf." He was more upbeat than I had recently heard, and he was looking for a miracle. But his hope would be short-lived.

In an attempt to garner favor with the publicity that might ensue, the emir made as much of a spectacle of the trip as possible. Any distraction was better than the attacks of the merchants. He gave me the use of his plane, a 747-8 BBJ, jumbo-size Boeing jet, for the trip across the Gulf and his armored Lincoln Town car to the airport. The state-sponsored news cameras were there as I climbed the ladder to the plane. I was becoming familiar with accompaniments of power, and I waved to the cameras. *Should I admit to myself that I enjoyed this?*

At the airport in Tehran, several officials in a black Mercedes picked me up on the tarmac and took me to the Laleh International Hotel and put me in the presidential suite. There was an anteroom, living room, full dining room, and bedroom with satin sheets. A large, locked wooden cabinet stood in the living room. I had been given the key; when I opened the cabinet, I saw it was filled with various brands of whiskey and vodka, totally against Islamic prohibitions. Dinner with lamb and pomegranate salad arrived in my suite promptly at seven o'clock.

The next morning, I was driven to the Sa'dabad Palace Complex, a group of ornate buildings built by the Qajar and Pahlavi monarchs. The royal families had been housed there in the nineteenth and early twentieth century. The many palaces of the complex, now mostly museums, connected the country's remarkable past with its possible future. Before seeing Zarif, the attendant showed me the Green Palace with its Hall of Mirrors. The light reflected from the small pieces of glass in the hall formed a remarkable display of mirrored colors, and I was appropriately complimentary to my guide. Then we went to the White Palace, with its three arched windows over the entry porch, to meet with the president. I was ushered into the cypress-paneled meeting room with its gold-painted trim. The appearance of wealth was still necessary for the strong leader. I wondered at the meetings that had preceded ours over the years. Perhaps the 1979 American hostage situation had been discussed here.

Zarif began first, and I had no opportunity to give my plea. "I want your support," he began. *Already the meeting was upside down. I thought I was the one coming for help.*

"Support for what and why my support?"

Zarif knew everything: why I was there, about the "Persian traitor" in Kuwait, everything. He bypassed all that and proceeded with his concerns. "I want you to support the end of the theocracy. This may be slow in coming, but it will come. The Ayatollah must leave. He's an old man and all he wants is the money, more than anything else. We're arranging an escape for him to Paris. His people will go with him. He has enough money to last them all forever. The information we have about his scandalous acquisition of the funds is remarkably precise and accurate. He knows that if we released it, he would be finished" He paused to drink his tea. *My thoughts ran wild. Why should he expect my support?* I soon found out. "We know your involvement in all this. Have you considered it might have been your friend who helped Khameini line his pockets?" He looked at me and was silent for a moment. He didn't have to say he knew of my involvement with Khadim's fortune and *his* clandestine efforts in lining his own pockets too. "Never mind. Your Persian friend in Kuwait has nothing to fear from me or the Ayatollah. You can tell him so." *Khadim was never actually named in our conversation.*

"But what can I do? I have no say over what happens in Iran. I have no role here at all."

"In time, you're going to be leader of the states on your side of the Gulf. All we ask of you is that you do not interfere in our affairs. We want peace. You've known our people. You know we can be a great country." He leaned forward. "You're a Christian. You know what's happening on both sides of the Gulf with your strange faith. We can't restrain it. We've tried. There's no point in the government trying to stop the movement anymore. Let's agree on that point anyway." I nodded. I couldn't speak. *Had the Lord done all this? I had not seen it as clearly as Zarif.*

The movement of the Spirit had preceded me. I was amazed by what I was hearing. "Shout for joy in the Lord, O you righteous! Praise befits the upright. Give thanks to the Lord with the lyre; make melody to him with the harp of ten strings! Sing to him a new song; play skillfully on the strings, with loud shouts" (Psalm 33:1-3). *I couldn't sing at that moment, but the impulse was there, and I suddenly felt freed. Why had I been so slow of spirit? It no longer mattered.*

"So now you've heard it all. You're here because there's no one else to lead, no one else to call on. You're now the Secretary General of the GCC. The emirs are going to run. The Ayatollah is going to run too."

As I departed the palace, I finally sang out praises to God out loud in Arabic. The song of Miriam and Moses came to me: "The horse and his rider he has thrown into the sea" (Exodus 15:21b). Those on the street didn't understand. I heard them say *divooneh*, which means insane in Farsi. Indeed.

That night before my departure, I walked to the Jama'-at e-Rabbani Church, run by the Assemblies of God, on Takht Jamshid Avenue. The church was now one of the largest in Tehran. The ushers at the door wore business suits and greeted each new arrival warmly. On a Wednesday night the church was full. There were two services in separate sanctuaries, one conducted in Farsi (Persian) and one in Armenian. Attendees occupied all the seats and later arrivals stood in the back of the church. The average age of the attendees, apart from the children, appeared to be about thirty.

Before this, the Assemblies of God in Iran had been subject to great persecution because of their large numbers of Muslim conversions. Now, they displayed a new air of freedom. "For the Lord, the Most High, is to be feared, a great king over all the earth. He subdued peoples under us, and nations under our feet" (Psalm 47:2-3) The kingdoms of the earth, the sand-earth of the Gulf, had again been subdued.

This was a church of converts, and many of them had likely been Shia Muslims. The pattern was now clear. I felt the obligation to report to Emir Nawaf on his earlier theological question about whether or not there could be a resolution of the Sunni-Shia conflict. He would not like the answer.

CHAPTER 16

END AND BEGINNING

When I returned, I stopped to see Qasar (Khadim), telling him, "You're safe. You have nothing to worry about from Khamenei and his cronies. They're too busy with their own problems, and Zarif is more progressive than any other politician in the Gulf. I think he'll be viewed someday as a great leader. Perhaps you'll eventually want to return to Tehran." Karim looked on, standing with hands on his hips, his mouth partially open.

He responded, "No way. We are never going back." But he collapsed in his chair with relief. He shouted, "Najwa, please come and hear this." His wife swiftly emerged from the kitchen. For the first time ever, she joined us. She was not covered.

I went through the same explanation to her, and they embraced. She began crying as she held him and stroked his back. Of the two, she was the comforter.

Then I told them about what I saw at the large church in Tehran. "The church was filled with young people. No one was interfering with their worship. I think most were new converts from Islam too. It was clear that many were unsure how to conduct themselves in a Christian worship service. They were looking around at each other, hoping to imitate what they saw in others. They were all probably formerly Shias."

Najwa opened up immediately, and for a moment took the center. "I'm a free woman here in Kuwait. I dress as I want. I speak to men if I choose. My children see me as a person separate from Karim. This freedom is from Jesus. Only the Shia, by the Spirit, could make this choice, not the Sunni."

I was still standing as I shook my head in amazement. "I see what's happened with you here in Kuwait. It's more than I had hoped for." I wasn't prepared for their rapid changes. Najwa invited me to sit, and took the chair next to Karim across from me.

She continued, and it was same theme I had heard from Imam Khatami, but with more added to it, "It's a matter of authority. For the Sunni, earthly authority surrounds them. This Sunni mullah is wiser than the next mullah. And the consensus of the community is the new truth every day. The Shias have always looked to a higher authority, an authority outside their experience. For a thousand years it has been the story of the hidden twelfth imam. This is the central difference, looking to a source outside our immediate experience. Shias have always been searching for the one with authority." Karim was quiet, content to let Najwa explain. "And the word of authority has now echoed through our people. That Shias could accept such an outside informant was the beginning of the turning. You may ask, 'Who is the authority, the informant?' The answer is, 'It is not a man.' The informant has been the Spirit of God speaking to our hearts. The Spirit enabled us to accept there would be a *return* of one who saves. Isa, Jesus, of course, has done the rest."

I listened without speaking and wondered where this woman had gotten her depth.

She completed her brief discourse, "And of course the Shia tend to be poor, more so than the Sunni. God used that too. Karim and I aren't poor, but He saved us anyway."

My mother's favorite psalm came to me. "Some wandered in desert wastes, finding no way to a city to dwell in; hungry and thirsty, their soul fainted within them. Then they cried to the Lord in their trouble, and he delivered them from their distress" (Psalm 107:4-6). I saw, in this desert place, the journey of the Shia and my own as well.

Najwa nodded to me, rose to leave the room, and said to Karim, "He must come tomorrow night, and he must bring Tahara." Najwa had assumed an advanced role, and Karim did not object.

The next evening, we drove to Khalidiya for the next phase of the venture. I wondered why Tahara's presence was requested. We were anxious in anticipation of the evening, but we didn't know the purpose of the visit.

When we arrived, there were two others present in the study waiting for us: Anand Kulabali and Imam Ali Khatami. I had not seen Khatami since he tried to explain Shiism to me. His beard was now white, and he looked unwell. The changes had added years to his appearance. Najwa brought tea, and Tahara and I waited for the evening to develop.

Imam Khatami began, "I told you what it means to be a Shia. Much has happened since we spoke. I told you we Shias look to the return of the last Mahdi. Today many of us know that Isa is the last Mahdi. There have been dreams and there has been truth-speaking, and now we know the truth."

Kulabali picked up the theme. "We were always the People of the Return. Now we are the People of the Return of Isa. I could have told you more when we met in the Seychelles, but you would have known too much too soon. However, when you needed me in Yemen, I was there. You must have suspected then that there was more to the story than I had revealed."

Tahara and I were both feeling unwell, dizzy with the speed of this information. I could see the concern in Tahara's eyes. *Why were we being brought further into this? Why should their risk be ours?* Once again, God swept us along.

Tahara got right to the point, "Why are Yusef and I here together?"

Kulabali continued. "Tahara, you still have connections with Al Jazeera. You still write an occasional piece for them. Now the time has come to tell the world about the People of the Return of Isa." Tahara and I expressed our concern about the danger. Kulabali went on. "This is the time. The emirs are going to leave. The change is coming swiftly now. There won't be time or effort available to hurt us. Those who might otherwise be our enemies are too concerned about their money right now. We must act."

After an hour and a half, we adjourned to dinner. Kulabali enjoyed filling in Tahara with the details of my "romance" with the ram in the back seat of our pickup in Yemen. The closeness we experienced with these four, who were former Shia Muslims, exceeded my expectations. Imam Khatami gave thanks to Isa, and we began the meal featuring potato patties with garlic chives (*kuku sibzamini*) and stuffed eggplant. It was as if I were back in Tehran for dinner. Tahara was as overcome as I was.

As was the custom, we left shortly after the meal. We had our fill of both food and new information. What next?

As we drove home, I reminded Tahara of another psalm. Usually the spiritual direction came from her, but tonight I was first to capsulize the events. "The Lord reigns; he is robed in majesty; the Lord is robed; he has put on strength as his belt; Yes, the world is established; it shall never be moved" (Psalm 93:1-2*). I longed to be certain of the security God provided.*

The next morning Tahara e-mailed her article about our meeting to Al Jazeera. The major news systems picked up the story: "Mass Conversions of Shia to Jesus."

###

I phoned the emir and drove to the Seif Palace. There were no attendants at the gate. The building was in disarray and packing boxes jammed the hallways. The emir was just getting dressed. I met him in the anteroom to his bedroom. He dispensed with the formality of kingship.

His personal bags were being packed. Paintings I had not seen were being crated. Most of them would be considered "against Islam" because of their depiction of the human form. Then, I saw it in the corner. The artist had marvelously captured the female figure in angles rather than curves. Nawaf saw me looking at the painting. "No, it's not *Les Demoiselles d'Avignon*, but it is by Picasso. It's another version of the same subject matter. But it has only been seen by a handful of people. You're the first Kuwaiti to see it. It cost me 200 million dinars." Or it had cost the people of Kuwait 200 million dinars.

"Your Highness, I've come to complete the assignment you gave me on reconciliation between the Sunni and Shia. I must tell you there is no ground for any such agreement. They have been separated by history and belief for centuries. There is no philosophical basis for compromise, and now the Shia are becoming Christians."

Nawaf responded, "I saw your wife's post on the Al Jazeera website. It doesn't matter anymore to me. I won't be here. Now it's your problem. All the emirs will be gone soon. My only joy in this is thinking of the difficulty you'll have with the various elected officials. They'll all want it their way. The people of the Gulf aren't ready for democracy. I hope you enjoy getting what you wanted." He had slipped to sarcasm.

I still did not fully understand what God had done. Surely there must be alternatives that exclude me from the picture. I saw now that God was too great to need me. "Praise the Lord! I will give thanks to the Lord with my whole heart, in the company of the upright, in the congregation. Great are the works of the Lord, studied by all who delight in them" (Psalm 111:1-2). Thus, I pondered the direction in front of me.

But there was a need for the GCC to meet immediately, and as the Secretary General, it was my responsibility to set the meeting. The states of the Gulf, except for Saudi Arabia and Iran, would soon have no functioning governments, no recognized leaders.

Tahara and I and little Ephraim flew down to the Marsa Malaz Kempinski Hotel in Doha for the GCC meeting. She had questioned the wisdom of her trip with the baby, but I responded, "I want you to be there in your homeland for the writing of the new document that will bind the Gulf together. For the first time, Tahara, I feel safe in God's hands."

Since the governments of the Gulf were in disarray, the members of our group were now without any sort of designated authority. We were suddenly our own authority. Two of the participants had changed. Fareed was now representing Qatar. The Qatari emir had apparently made the change at the last moment. Anand Kulabali appeared as the representative of Ras Al Khaimah from the Emirates. Once again he appeared at the right time.

One by one the GCC representatives shared the conditions in their various states. The Omani member's recitation was typical. Talib Al-Ajman said, "We're glad the thief and his entourage are gone, but there is nothing to replace them. The people have no way of making or implementing a decision. There are no acute needs now, but they will arise. And we have enemies, or potential enemies, on our doorsteps. There are the Wahhabists in Saudi, and there is Iran across the Gulf. If they continue their attempts at political disruption around the globe, we will be in the middle of two fighting giants."

The Bahraini representative echoed the same fears. "The Saudis have come into our state before, and they can easily cross the bridge into our country again unless we're united." The King Fahd Causeway connecting the two countries had been built for peaceful purposes, but it was also a potential route for invasion.

The conclusion among the group was that both Saudi Arabia and Iran were potential threats. I knew Iran was not.

Kulabali added, "The changes we're seeing now will eclipse our fears of yesterday. The Shias are changing faster than anyone expected. We're turning to Jesus. It's happening on both sides of the Gulf." Kulabali's courage outstripped my own for the moment, but I was accustomed to others outdistancing me in that arena. Once again, Anand was there for me. He had appeared at the meeting as if by chance, but of course, it was not by chance.

Fareed began, "The only avenue for us is to unite. We must be one if we're to resist the Saudis and the Persians. We must distinguish ourselves from them. Many of the elite have said we're 'not ready for democracy.'" I remembered Nawaf's comment. "It seems we have no other choice. The first step is to form a federation of states. We must have a document that can be offered as a referendum to do that."

For the next morning's meeting I asked Tahara and Hibah to sit as guests of the council. I summarized the morning meeting with the conclusion that we now had the task of writing a constitution for the federation. "I propose the principles that must be included. Each state must elect its own representative government or parliament. There must be no parliamentary monarchy, that is no monarchy. Those parliaments will choose the members of the GCC Council. All the citizens of the member states should vote on the Secretary General position. Freedom of religion must be guaranteed. There can be no penalty for leaving Islam, or any other religion."

There were staunch, conservative Sunnis among the council members. Yet they either kept silent or openly agreed. Events had cancelled any objection.

The psalms of praise had by now replaced my songs of lament and imprecation. "Not to us, O Lord, not to us, but to your name give glory, for the sake of your steadfast love and your faithfulness! Why should the nations say, 'Where is their God?' Our God is in the heavens; he does all that he pleases" (Psalm 155:1-3). I prayed my actions pleased God. The events of the next few days were critical, and I was the *de facto* leader.

By the next evening, Tahara, Ephraim and I we were having dinner in the Al Sufra restaurant of the Marsa Malaz. As we ate the Lebanese food before us, tabbouleh, hummus, and lamb kebabs, we experienced a novel sense of freedom. The Lord had freed us.

In the meetings we talked for hours about the constitution and what it should say. Tahara and Hibah listened to the discussions, took careful notes, and composed the document. Hibah's skills as an attorney and Tahara's writing ability meshed quite well. (And they were no longer competing in the same house.)

The emirs had all abdicated and resided in Ta'if. They had each departed their countries on the same day. The emirs took up residence in the cool, high mountain, vacation city of the Saudi royal family. The city was formerly known for its grapes, pomegranate, figs, roses, and honey. Now it was known for this gathering of the former emirs of Kuwait, Oman, Bahrain, Qatar, and the seven Emirates too. The Saudi king was the twelfth monarch, and therefore Ta'if was soon known as the City of Honey and the Twelve Kings. Ta'if was elevated in status. Due to the remarkable infusion of funds and the large retinue of servants of the former Gulf leaders, Whole Foods and Wal-Mart opened stores. The Whole Foods meat section was entirely *halal* (meaning the animals were slaughtered in the proper Islamic fashion).

By mid-July the constitution was ready for presentation to the citizens of the member states. We set the referendum date for Tuesday, September 15, 2026, the International Day of Democracy, with the knowledge that those who departed during the summer heat of the Gulf would have returned by then. Tahara wisely commented, "Don't tell them women wrote their constitution." The new constitution was approved by ninety percent of the voters. They really had little choice. The Gulf States, other than Saudi Arabia and Iran, were now united by a new day of personal freedom. Sharia law was no longer a part of the legal system. We adopted a model of law based on the principles and precedents used in English common law. This change alone was a miracle, and it was accomplished with remarkable speed. With passage of the referendum, I resigned as Secretary General to pave the way for elections.

The tide of conversions to Jesus, particularly among the Shias, now proceeded unimpeded. We flew back to Kuwait and attended Thawab's church. For the first time in my life I lifted up my hands in worship. This had been standard procedure for Tahara, and she looked at me and smiled.

The Kuwaiti Parliament nominated me for Secretary General. I made no attempt to campaign. Two others mounted campaigns for the office: Ali Al-Bader from Abu Dhabi and Hussein Al-Azari from Oman. Each criticized the other heavily for reasons that were never entirely clear. I received eighty percent of the vote from the participating Gulf States.

As the now officially elected Secretary General of the new Federation of Gulf States, I negotiated formal mutual protection agreements with both Saudi Arabia and Iran. They were eager to comply. Mohammed Bin Salman spoke with a derisive tone, "I thank Allah for your victories. You must protect me from ISIL and the Persians." Both Iran and Saudi Arabia had their own bigger problems. The world was closing in on them.

The flood of Christian converts continued both in Iran and in the Federation. The statistics of religious affiliation in the Gulf were rendered meaningless. The demographers couldn't keep up. "Praise the Lord! For it is good to sing praises to our God; for it is pleasant, and a song of praise is fitting. The Lord builds up Jerusalem; he gathers the outcasts of Israel. He heals the brokenhearted and binds up their wounds" (Psalm 147:1-3). Now I saw that, in God's eyes, we were the exiles who were gathered.

Esau was the exile who was not gathered. I had heard that, after his second deportation back to America, he was caught in attempts to hack into several hedge funds. The fund managers were not as forgiving as the emir, and he fled for his life from the justice. *Where was he now?*

As attractive as I was said to be, as capable as many saw me, I saw that God had directed the events. He had orchestrated the collected personalities. There was Yacoub, my father, whom God converted at the Wadi Batin. There was Rabea, my mother, with her wonderful mind and converted spirit, who taught me, no, really forced me, to know the Psalms. There was Hibah, the image of my mother, with her keen mind. There was Tahara, who dared to love me and cry for me. There was Binyamin who foiled Esau with his computer skills. There was Thawab, the half-brother whom I resented, who became the leader of the church in Kuwait. There was the strange one, Kulabali, who was there when I needed him. There was the imam, with his beloved Oreos, Ali Khatami, who saw the return of Isa as the key. There was Karim, the Persian bureaucrat and thief, who told me what I needed to know and came to Jesus along with his family.

It was God who put all this together, none other than Him. "Praise the Lord! Praise the Lord from the heavens; praise him in the heights! Praise him, all his angels; praise him, all his hosts! Praise him, sun and moon, praise him, all you shinning stars! Praise him, you highest heavens, and you waters above the heavens!" (Psalm 148:1-4). God did the work.

And as for me, I am only Yusef, prince of the sand.

IF YOU'RE A FAN OF THIS BOOK, WILL YOU HELP ME SPREAD THE WORD?

There are several ways you can help me get the word out about the message of this book...

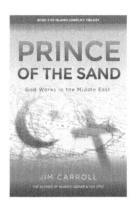

- Post a 5-Star review on Amazon.

- Write about the book on your Facebook, Twitter, Instagram – any social media you regularly use!

- If you blog, consider referencing the book, or publishing an excerpt from the book with a link back to my website. You have my permission to do this as long as you provide proper credit and backlinks.

- Recommend the book to friends – word-of-mouth is still the most effective form of advertising.

- Purchase additional copies to give away as gifts. You can do that by going to my website at: www.allfaithsoil.com

ENJOY THESE OTHER BOOKS BY JIM CARROLL

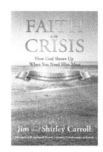 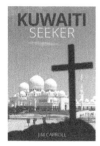 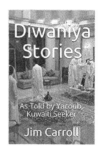 

Faith in Crisis – How God Shows Up When You Need Him Most, Kuwaiti Seeker, Hot Spot – A Turbulent Modern Story in an Ancient Land, Diwaniya Stories

amazon   BARNES&NOBLE

You can order these books from AMAZON & B&N or where ever you purchase your favorite books. You can also order these books from my website at: www.allfaithsoil.com

NEED A SPEAKER FOR YOUR NEXT PROGRAM?

Invite me to speak to your group or ministry. I have many years of public speaking experience. If you would like to have me speak to your group or at an upcoming event, please contact me at: www.allfaithsoil.com